GUNNER

Fire Lake – Book 5

M. Tasia

ALSO BY M. TASIA

The Boys of Brighton series

Gabe

Sam's Soldiers

Rick's Bear

Jesse

Coop

Travis

Grady

Vincent

Shadow

The Holidays

The Gates series

Saint

Finn

James

Joey

Bradley

Carlos

Sawyer

Trey

Fire Lake series

Brick

Fletcher

Shaw

Spencer

READERS ARE WILD
ABOUT FIRE LAKE

"What a great beginning to a series! Brick and Roman are perfect together. Add in the murder factor and some well trained military men and you have the makings of an awesome series. It was a well written story that kept me engaged from the first page. Cannot wait for Fletch, Spencer, and Shaw's book."
~I Love Books 2005 on Brick

"Fletcher is the latest in M. Tasia's Fire Lake series, a lineup of action-packed M/M romances that I LOVE. Fletcher Daniels is a retired Navy SEAL - handsome, brave, and loyal to the military brothers with whom he has formed a security company, and he finds himself drawn to the local sheriff. Elias Cooper is as sexy as he is protective, and he wants Fletch just as much. Just when they decide to see where this burning attraction will lead them, the new couple, along with Brick and the other guys, become immersed in a missing persons case that hits really close to home. Fletch and Elias are equally strong, passionate men with their own demons, and it makes them one hell of a fierce couple. The respect with which Tasia treats these super steamy love stories gives me all the feels, and those heart-tugging aww moments, the sexy bits, and the suspense make it REALLY difficult for me to wait for the next installment. Once again, such amazing work, M. Tasia!"
~Shannon Williams on Fletcher

"I am really enjoying this series and I look forward to more books to come. I like the nature of these stories. A suspense story along with a romance. I like that the romances are low angst and missing the usual miscommunication or martyr tropes a lot of suspense romances seem to have. I think this author may have created a new sub-genre...a light and fluffy suspense romance if that's possible!

The suspense part of the story has enough intrigue to keep you guessing and the teensiest bit anxious while the romance part of the story is pretty instalove and mostly smooth sailing without cliched complications. We get a loving, caring relationship that we see gradually develop into more. The emotions are always a key part of the developing relationships helping us to see the men. We have new characters added in this book so I look forward to seeing how they fit in with the group and what their stories are. Looking forward to the next book".
~Beth I-L on Shaw

"The men of Fire Lake are embroiled in several mysteries at once. What starts as a simple case of a missing girl turns into shadowy characters and government secrets. Once again, the team works well together providing help to the innocent and finding love in the process. Rick's past was heartbreaking, but his relationship with Spence was sweet as they worked together. I loved how the team accepted him and his quirky behaviors."
~Book Addiction on Spencer

EVERYONE LOVES THE BOYS OF BRIGHTON

"I loved this book and I love this town. I hope there's going to be more."
—Melissa Lemons on *Gabe*

"An amazing read that was filled with lust, love, crazy hot sex, danger, action and so much more This is the first book I have read in this series but I will definitely be reading more in the future."
—Gay Book Reviews on *Sam's Soldiers*

"I was crazy impressed that the author made me teary over the ending of a relationship that I shouldn't have even been invested in. I didn't yet know these characters yet the author made me hurt for them. That takes some mad writing skills!"
—Love Bytes Reviews

"Jesse and Royce together have my heart. Jesse has it all by himself."
—The Book Junkie Reads on *Jesse*

"So much action, intrigue, drama and angst for the long awaited story of Grady and Ben. This was worth the wait. Sexy and sweet. I can't wait for the next."
—SamD on *Grady*

"I knew this one would be my favorite to date! There was something about Vincent that said awesome then came Tristan."
—Booky on *Vincent*

"This installment of the Boys of Brighton was so good! I loved Shadow and Randy 's story I was hooked from the first page to the last. This book was definitely worth the wait!"

—AG on *Shadow*

"I have loved this series from the very first story and this holiday novella is simply perfect. We get a glimpse of all our couples and what is happening in their lives while the holidays explode around them. I cannot wait for more!"
—bookobsessed on *The Holidays*

ANOTHER BIG LOVE – THE GATES

"Ms. Tasia has done it again! This is Saint's story, for readers of the Brighton Boys, you'll know he needs a break! After being forced to become a plastic surgeon by his father, he rebels by assisting people in 3rd world countries, which puts him in the position to be kidnapped and tortured. You really feel for him, that's for sure! Max is the perfect man for poor Saint's battered soul, not that he doesn't have his own issues! Overall, this was engaging, steady paced and chock full of all the feels!"
—Avid Reader on *Saint*

"Finn and Miguel stole my heart. This is a great Sunday afternoon read. Finn's character jumped off the page as his story developed through each chapter. I loved reading his truth and watching him and Miguel find their home in each other."
—K.A. Brown on *Finn*

"This is really a great series and I def recommend it. I loved James and Ross, it was a rough start for the two, but they worked it out. I can't wait for more, love everything M. TASIA writes!"
—TammyKay on *James*

"I may have my new favorite book couple of the series. Joey and Sam just have that something special. At one point I was ugly crying

but it was a good ugly cry if that makes any sense. I really love the series and I can't wait for her next installment!!"
—Vine Voice on *Joey*

"This author is really talented and I love her series, this one and the Boys of Brighton. Her characters are so well drawn and I can really get into the stories. I especially loved Eric in this particular book. I'm hoping Clay the rookie will be the next book. Keep 'em coming!"
—Rosemary on *Bradley*

"Two men with damaged souls come together and find love. A tried and true formula that works well here, especially when working with two lovable characters like Carlos and Clay. Carlos especially was interesting to me - the contrast of his appearance to his gentle nature, a true gentle giant. And Clay being all protective of the much larger, but more gentle man - so sweet! I really liked this story and am looking forward to more of The Gates now."
—Valeen on *Carlos*

"Sawyer is the newest addition to The Gates series. The book is very emotional, sweet, funny, romantic, and these two are great together. I look forward to every book in this series."
—Elaine Gray on *Sawyer*

"This book has all the feels and pulls the reader right in. It was wonderful to see how the two of them went from adversaries to respect to falling in love. You won't want to miss their story to see the path they travel and if there is a HEA waiting at the end. There is much more going on here, but hopefully this is enough to convince you that you will not want to miss this one."

~Emily Pennington on *Trey*

www.BOROUGHSPUBLISHINGGROUP.com

PUBLISHER'S NOTE: This is a work of fiction. Names, characters, places and incidents either are the product of the author's imagination or are used fictitiously. Any resemblance to actual events, locales, business establishments or persons, living or dead, is coincidental. Boroughs Publishing Group does not have any control over and does not assume responsibility for author or third-party websites, blogs or critiques or their content.

GUNNER
Copyright © 2023 M. Tasia

ISBN: 978-1-957295-33-6

To my family for their unwavering support.
I love all of you to the moon and back.

Acknowledgments

I want to thank my ARC team for their time and effort in helping me bring the best stories to everyone I can. Thank you, Pattie, Heather, Stacie, Victoria, Natasha, Mildred, Michelle, and Shannon. You ladies rock.

Gunner

CHAPTER ONE

Gunner

"Seriously, get the fuck out. *Sakra*."

"Not until I've done what I came here to do," Conor stated, undeterred. "What does *sakra* mean?"

Gunner didn't answer. Most of the team knew what he meant. Well, some of the time. When Spencer chuckled, Gunner figured Spence got that he'd said *damn it*.

Trying a different tactic, Gunner asked. "Brick, can you do something here?"

"Nope." Brick shook his head. "Don't drag me into Conor's grandmother's mojo crap." He took another gulp of coffee.

Coward, Gunner thought.

"He's not doing any harm. Let him finish," Roman said with a shrug from behind his lowered newspaper.

"Ugh. You're all in on this craziness," Gunner muttered. How was he the only sound-minded one of the group? Typically, he was the team member everyone else thought was nuts. "*Sileny*. We're all screwed if I'm the sane one."

When stressed, which, given his chosen profession, was most of the time, Gunner frequently peppered his speech and thoughts with Czech curses.

"Any extra help is welcome if it means keeping your nephew, Ben, out of the in-laws' hands," Rick said as he set a tray full of French toast down in the center of the kitchen table.

After months of battering him for feeding them twigs and barks, Rick relented and became more open to adding other foods to their diet. Although, Gunner was certain, the bread was whole grain and the eggs free range, and that the organic maple syrup was shipped from a special grove of trees in Canada.

It'd been over a month since they'd returned to the lake house after dealing with a few loose ends in the Hammon case, and Conor O'Brian was still hanging around driving Gunner up the wall. The sniper had been the definition of patience until Conor showed up.

As for the Hammon case and the Noah Project, there still was no information on Ellen Hammon's brother, though they'd determined the baby boy was alive, as opposed to what Elise, Ellen's late mother, had been told at the time of his birth.

The boy had been genetically modified just like his sister, but there was no information on his whereabouts or the extent of the mutation.

Most concerning was the boy wasn't the only one missing from the children born because of the evil program. The files the team had discovered had fifty kids, but there might be more since there was no indication the "project" had stopped. There could be well over fifty people of various ages walking around with mutated genes, and no one knew what that meant for those children.

"Don't you think you repaid me when you threw your body on top of me back at that storage facility?" Gunner asked. Had shit gone sideways, they'd both be dead right now.

Conor was a private investigator who'd been hired by Ben's biological father's parents, Lisa and Frank Wells, to find Gunner so they could serve him with court papers. They were contesting the custody designation made in his dead sister's will. They were trying to take Ben, who was almost five years old, away from his Uncle Gunner.

Ben's biological father, Jason, had signed away all his parental rights when Ben was born, and until recently, Gunner had never heard from Jason's side of the family.

After sharing the facts with Conor, the guy had decided not to follow through with his assignment and had sided with Gunner and Ben. Why he'd attached himself to the team, and was here at the lake house, was a complete mystery, and Gunner hoped he'd leave soon. As for the rest of the team, they'd welcomed Conor into the fold as he'd used his own body to protect Gunner from a bullet.

"No. That had nothing to do with fixing the situation with the in-laws. It was simply the right thing to do given the situation," Conor stated. "If you'd given me a gun, we wouldn't've been put in that position."

"If it hadn't been you, another PI would have taken the job. For all we know, another has. In any case, I would've been served with those papers, and I still might be. You owe me nothing." What would it take to convince this guy to leave? "And I'm still not giving you a gun, *bibec*."

Conor grinned. "I already have a gun since Brick returned mine. And as for this case, my mam won't forgive me if I let this go."

The guy talking about his grandmother reminded Gunner of his estranged family, which was never a good road to travel. Other than his sister, no one else had accepted Gunner when he came out. Long-held beliefs had followed his family from what was then Czechoslovakia, and those beliefs and traditions were set in stone. Them knowing he was gay was the end of their already tenuous relationship.

While Gunner never regretted his decision to walk away, he couldn't say he didn't miss having his family. Initially, he was surprised his parents weren't suing him for custody of Ben. Then again, they'd never fight his sister's wishes.

"Is your grandmother still alive?" Fletch asked as he took his seat beside Elias.

"Eighty-six and going strong," Conor said with a smile. "Grandma Jackie lives on the Jersey shore with my Aunt Viv."

"Don't you have a life to get back to?" Spence asked while eying Gunner.

"Nothing that can't wait, as I'm sure you've already researched." Conor smiled at their information specialist, knowing full well Conor had been thoroughly vetted before ever being allowed near Fire Lake.

Spence shrugged before grinning wide. "It's my job to know."

"And I respect that," Conor replied.

The group quieted as soft footsteps sounded on the stairs, and moments later, Ben appeared from around the corner.

"'Morning, buddy," Gunner said as he opened his arms for Ben to get his morning bear hug.

"'Morning, Uncle Gunner," Ben said, wrapping his tiny arms around Gunner's neck. Nothing could ever replace the feeling of pure love he got from his nephew. In those precious moments, he felt his sister was with him.

He stood with Ben in his arms, lifting the little dude high into the air with a happy laugh. Gunner understood the need to be on higher ground with all the large men in the house.

The rest of the team wished Ben good morning while Gunner air-planed him into his booster seat as Gunner made sounds of plane engines and squealing tires. Ben loved it and laughed with a child's unbridled joy.

"'Morning, Ben," Conor said as he sat beside the little dude.

"'Morning, Uncle Conor," Ben replied.

When the hell had Conor turned into Uncle anything?

The guy was wheedling his way into their lives at the lake house, and Gunner didn't like it. Conor wasn't part of their team, but now wasn't the time to discuss that. Gunner sat on the other side of Ben and began filling his nephew's plate with fruit, a piece of French toast, and turkey bacon.

"Orange juice, buddy?" Conor asked while holding up the juice container before Gunner could grab it.

"Yes, please." Ben smiled wide. He'd been doing more of that lately, which gave Gunner hope his nephew's pain from losing his mom was easing. Though Gunner knew from experience, it would never fully go away.

Conor filled Ben's new Spider-Man cup the team had bought for him along with bags filled with clothes and games. Ben's room was brimming with stuff that couldn't fit into his dresser or closet while they were busy repairing a neglected room to make into a playroom to house his and Julia's son Matthew's growing number of toys. As was their way, the team had gone all out and had bought all sorts of things for Ben to make him feel welcome, and so he wouldn't want for anything.

Gunner finished filling Ben's plate, and the noise level in the kitchen dropped to the sounds of cutlery hitting plates and sounds of "mmm" as everyone dug into their food.

Gunner had to hand it to Rick. He'd found a way to make healthy foods taste great as he incorporated them into their delicious everyday meals. Since discovering the reason behind Rick's need to feed them super-healthy foods, the team had become more accommodating. Losing someone dear to heart disease was crushing and explained a lot.

"This is killer French toast," Fletch said before digging his fork into the pile on the tray to take a second helping.

"Thanks. It's a new recipe Julia and I have been working on." Rick beamed as Spence pulled him close.

"Wouldn't hurt if you tried your hand at *buchty*," Gunner said. He'd missed those jam-filled pastries his mother used to make. He was a pretty damn good cook, but he never could quite repeat her recipe.

Rick looked thoughtful as he scrolled on his phone to figure out what Gunner said. "Oh, pastries. Okay. I'll look at the recipe and see what I can do. Traditionally, Czech food is carb-heavy with lots of creams and fats, but I'm up for a challenge."

"Great." Gunner appreciated that Rick would try, and odds were, the result would be stupendous. Gunner knew the food he'd grown up eating wasn't light and particularly health-friendly. In his mother's kitchen, you could never have too much sauce, gravy, or cream.

"Are we still laying the foundation for the cottages today?" Elias, Fletch's man and the local sheriff, asked. "I have the next two days off, so I should be around to help."

"Yeah. I'd like to have the forms built by lunch," Brick said. "The weather's supposed to hold for the next five days, which'll give the concrete time to set."

Since the lake house was well on its way to being fully renovated, and since the team kept expanding, the group required more living space. Brick was down with adding the cottages, which would be bigger than tiny houses, but would blend in well to the wooded property fronting Fire Lake.

An arborist had come out to help them decide which trees to remove or relocate without harming the small forest surrounding the lake house. After getting the arborist's recommendations, Brick worked with an architect and found he'd have enough room for seven moderate-size cottages. One would be for Gunner and Ben, another for Fletch and Elias, and one for Julia and her son Matthew. Shaw, Kyle, and Bryan had settled on Bryan's ranch, which meant Spence and Rick were the only other couple who'd live in the original lake house with Roman and Brick.

Gunner had overheard Brick saying his great-aunt Sophia would've loved all the changes he'd made to the property. Looking around the table, Gunner thought she'd approve of more than the structural changes. Life and love were returning to the lake house, and that was a good thing.

Gunner looked forward to the day when he and Ben would have a home of their own, and he'd work his ass off to see that happen. He could imagine Ben's room already, bunk beds, of course, so Matthew could come for sleepovers, and the boys would have enough space for all their toys.

He hoped his sister would agree with his choices for her son. Gunner was in foreign waters when it came to parenting, but he'd be damned if he'd fail her or Ben. As far as he was concerned, raising Ben was his new mission in life. The most important mission he'd ever had, and he refused to fail, even with the in-laws circling like vultures.

"Rick, man, you got a handle on this menu thing," Elias said. "I can't tell if this is good for me or not."

"Trust me, it's good for you," Rick said with a smile. "Make sure you eat some fruit along with your French toast, Sheriff."

Elias chuckled and scooped another spoonful of Rick's strawberry and raspberry fruit bowl onto his plate. "Happy cook, happy life."

"You got that right," Conor agreed before following suit.

"Suck-up," Gunner mumbled, causing Conor to smile even wider.

"What does suck-up mean, Uncle Gunner?" Ben asked, eliciting chuckles from the team.

Sometimes Gunner forgot to censor his mouth when Ben was around, and once again it was coming back to bite him in the ass.

"Well, um," he began, with no idea how to finish that sentence.

"You see, Ben," Conor interjected, "that term is used when people go out of their way to make someone happy."

"Wait a minute," Gunner interrupted. "Those people go out of their way for their gain, not to make someone happy."

"Not the way I meant it," Conor shot back.

"Yeah, right," Gunner growled.

Ben looked between them, obviously still waiting for an explanation, and Gunner finally came up with one. "It's a big person word you'll understand when you're older."

"Okay," Ben said and returned to his breakfast, but continued to watch Gunner and Conor.

Gunner shot Conor a "do not mess with me" glare before scanning the table to find everyone else watching them. "What?"

"You're like an old married couple. It's weird," Rick answered.

Gunner looked over at Conor and glared even harder. "Not a chance."

"I like my French toast, Uncle Rick." Ben beamed before happily continuing, "I'm a suck-up too."

Slowly, Gunner closed his eyes and buried his head in his hands. The rest of the table roared with laughter, so he had no choice but to play along. He rubbed the top of his little guy's head covered in dark hair like his and Ben's mom's.

"You're a good kid," he said. "Now eat up. Matthew and Julia should be here shortly." As soon as their cottage was finished, Julia was moving them from town to the lake house permanently.

Ben dug into his fruit without another word. He and Matthew had become fast friends and did everything together. From fishing to their love of toys that transformed into robots. Both had growing collections and spent hours playing together on the porch or under the large tree beside the lake house. In the fall, they'd be attending kindergarten together.

As if summoned, Julia's car pulled into the driveway. After Ben chewed his last piece of strawberry, he asked, "Can I go, Uncle Gunner?"

"Yeah, kid. Go have fun," Ben scrambled off his booster and reached for one of his robot toys as he headed for the door.

The moment he was out of earshot, Gunner turned to Conor. "We need to get one thing of many things straight, muthafucka. I'm raising Ben. You need to stay the hell out of our lives."

Before Conor could reply, Gunner stormed out the garden doors and headed to the worksite.

A couple of hours pounding a hammer was exactly what he needed.

CHAPTER TWO

Conor

Conor's back was aching, but he'd be damned if he'd stop. With his resolve set, he hoisted another load of two-by-fours onto his shoulder and carried them over to the other side of the property. Watching the other guys haul serious amounts of weight around like they were lifting balsa wood made him even more conscious of his lack of physical strength.

Although he possessed the strength of a normal six-foot healthy male, these men were not normal. Well, not the team members and the sheriff. They were superhuman or some shit because he was having a hard time keeping up.

Even Clancy "Gator" Hutch, retired Army and the local bar owner, was helping and seemed unaffected by the hard work and heat. Then to add insult to injury, the older former Marines known as "the fishing crew" showed up in one of their boats. Jeff, Tuck, Wreck, and Andy, as they were introduced, were holding up better than Conor. Must be because they'd all spent time in the military. What the hell did they feed them? Teach them?

After breakfast, Conor had been at it for hours, only stopping once to download a Czech translation app onto his phone. Conor was determined to figure out what the hell Gunner was saying.

As he wished he was lying under a tree with Molly, Jeff's chocolate Labrador Retriever, Conor dropped off his load of lumber and was about to turn around to go back to get more when Julia called to him from the house.

"Conor. Will you give me a hand with something?"

"Yes, ma'am. On my way," he replied, changed directions, and made for the house.

He took the stairs two at a time in case she needed help fast, but when he opened the door, he found her sitting at the kitchen table while Ben and Matthew played on the rug in the living room. The air-conditioned breeze wafted over his hot, tired body, and he couldn't stop the moan of relief that followed.

"What'd you need me to do?" he asked as he neared the kitchen.

"I need you to sit down before you fall down," she said while holding out a glass of iced tea.

The trickle of condensation running down the glass was his undoing, and he reached for the glass and gulped down its contents before collapsing onto the chair beside her.

"They can't be human," he gasped. "There's no way."

"Sometimes I wonder." She laughed. "Are you trying to get heat stroke?"

"No. I was trying to help."

"How are you with dishwashers?" she asked.

"I know my way around appliances."

"Good. Ours is acting like it has a cat stuck inside it every time I try to use it. The guys are so busy with the construction, I didn't want to bring it up to them." Julia pointed across the room at the broken appliance.

"So you thought you'd save my life while getting the dishwasher repaired," he summed it up.

"Exactly," she said with a grin.

"You're a fine woman," Conor groaned as he held the cold glass up against his forehead and tilted his head toward to the pile of lumber. "Thank god, that's over."

"Until tomorrow." She laughed. "When you'll do it all over again."

"Yep. I'm a glutton for punishment," he huffed before laughing.

"Toolbox is on the counter. Have at it while I refill your glass," she said as she reached for the pitcher.

"Thank you. You're a lifesaver." He wasn't joking. He'd been run ragged trying to keep up, and it wasn't even noon.

She gave him a shrewd look. "We'll see if you think so once you're done with that mess."

"Understood," he agreed, stood, and opened the toolbox. "I'll have to pull the dishwasher away from the wall."

The renovations on the kitchen hadn't been completed yet, so he wasn't worried he'd be damaging the flooring.

"Whatever you need to do to fix that hunk of junk long enough for the new appliances to arrive."

"You got it. I love puzzles."

This he could do. He was handy and could repair almost anything with an engine. Whenever something broke in his family, they called him to fix it. Fixing this would be a piece of cake. He pulled the machine into the center of the kitchen and got to work.

It wasn't long before Julia started peppering him with questions. "Why are you here? Why are you doing this?" Julia gestured to the wood pile, and then the dishwasher.

He looked over to the boys playing in the adjoining room. "How blunt do you want me to be?"

"Boys. Go on up to Ben's room and play there for a little while," Julia instructed.

"Okay," Matthew said before both boys ran up the stairs.

"I prefer as blunt as you need to be," she stated.

"Okay then. I'm doing this because I know what it feels like to be forced to stay with people who don't give a rat's ass about you."

"I don't understand. You talk about your family all the time. You sure sound like you love them and vice versa."

"I trust this will stay between the two of us." Most likely, Spence had probably ferreted out any and all information about Conor, and had surely told Brick, as he was the head of the team, but as far as Conor knew, no one else had his family information.

"Unless it endangers anyone here, I swear to silence." Julia crossed her heart. He liked her already. She was a straight shooter.

"I'm adopted." He hadn't said those words in a while, considering his family stated that he had been theirs since birth. It just took a bit longer to find him.

"Um, okay." That didn't seem to've hit her the way he expected, so he explained more fully.

"The foster homes I ended up in were looking for a paycheck without much fuss. As long as I stayed quiet, I went unnoticed most of the time."

"And you're not the quiet type," Julia stated.

He grinned. "Ah, no. When the social workers from CPS came to do their home checks, I'd fill them in on every meal I missed, the drugs sold, or how many junkies lived in the house. You never knew what you'd get when you were removed from one hellhole and placed in another. Later, when I came out as gay, it got harder. No one wanted the gay boy in their house, and those who did were scarier than the ones from before I came out."

With a slight hitch in her voice, she asked, "How old were you when you went into the system?"

Conor removed the back cover of the dishwasher and took a good look inside. "When you said this was old, you meant it. Got any bubblegum and bobby pins?"

"It's not that bad." Julia laughed as Conor had hoped. "How old were you?"

He took a deep breath. "I was three when it began."

"Did your parents die?" Julia asked softly.

"No. They didn't want me anymore. They surrendered me to the state." The truth hurt, but no matter how shitty, he'd been lucky and wound up with people who loved him.

Julia stood abruptly, causing Conor to rise at the noise of her tipped chair hitting the floor. She was headed his way fast, and before he knew what she was about, she'd wrapped her small arms around him and said in a shaky voice, "I'm so sorry they did that to you."

He wasn't sure what to do. She was in tears, and he was frozen to the spot. She finally released him at the same time the back door opened and Brick, Gunner, and Fletch walked in. *Shit.*

Julia turned and began drying her eyes, but the damage was done.

"What the fuck did you do to make Julia cry?" Gunner's tone was deadly as he stormed across the room.

"I-I didn't," Conor tried to spit out, but the guy was past listening.

Maybe he had this coming. Gunner placed his large hand on Conor's chest and pushed him away from Julia to the other side of the kitchen. Conor's feet got caught up in the area rug the kids had been playing on, and he lost his balance. He was headed for the floor before he could recover his balance.

He landed badly on his wrist and heard the snap before pain shot up his arm and had him gasping for breath.

Brick and Fletch looked stunned as Julia tried to explain, but the boys came down the stairs at the sound of commotion.

"Uncle Conor, why are you on the floor?" Ben asked.

"I wasn't looking where I was going and tripped on the rug. I'm okay. It was an accident." Conor tried to smile and be reassuring. "Everything's okay, buddy."

As the pain intensified, he felt like he was going to throw up. Gator came in looking confused and helped him to his feet. Conor was afraid he was going to pass out. He needed fresh air. Gator helped him make his way out the garden doors and onto the porch where Elias met him on the steps.

"What's going on?" Elias asked in that no-nonsense sheriff tone he probably used on all suspicious characters.

"A misunderstanding. Do you have a doctor in town?" Conor had to get medical attention.

Elias looked down at Conor's left arm and wrist. "Shit. That's gotta be broken."

"I'm pretty sure it is. Could you drive me in?" *Please say yes.*

"Sure. Of course," Elias said while looking from Conor to the house.

Conor followed Elias to his cruiser without looking up to see what the others were doing. As he sat in the passenger seat, Brick came running out of the house, and Elias went to meet him. Brick was probably telling Elias to leave Conor's sorry ass in town. Did they have a motel in Marshall?

Brick gazed over at the car, but Conor was in too much pain to decipher the look on the team leader's face. Elias ran back to the cruiser and hopped into the driver's seat.

"I'll have you to the doc in under ten." Then Elias turned on the lights and sirens.

"I'm not dying, man. It's only a broken wrist." There wasn't any need for bells and whistles.

"Put on your seatbelt," he ordered in a deep "don't fuck with me" sheriff voice.

"Yes, sir."

***

Gunner

For several hours, Gunner had been sitting on the porch waiting for Elias and Conor to return. Shame, as he'd never felt before, settled over him like a black fog. Julia had taken the boys to her house for a sleepover while he tried to figure out what the hell was wrong with him.

He never lost control. Never.

Until today.

What was it about Conor that brought out the worst in him? He'd found Julia in tears. Her chair was toppled over, and he saw red. There was no stopping him from removing the threat as quickly as possible.

But did he mean to hurt Conor?

That question was nagging at him, and Gunner didn't have the answer. Not yet, anyway.

True, he viewed the guy as a threat. After all, it wasn't that long ago that the dude was following him on behalf of a family who'd wanted nothing to do with Ben until Gunner had custody of him. Ben didn't even know them, but they believed the kid would be in better hands once away from gay influence.

Then again, Conor had risked his life to protect Gunner, and he'd repaid the guy by breaking his wrist.

Elias had called from the hospital to tell them Conor had two broken bones in his wrist that would require surgery to repair, which was scheduled for two days from now in order to let some of the swelling go down. Conor would have to wear a splint until the surgery, after which he'd be in a cast for six to eight weeks.

Gunner had to fix this. But how?

Then to add to the shitstorm, Julia explained why she'd been crying in the first place and why Conor was doing everything he was doing to protect Ben.

Yeah, Gunner knew he was a grade-A asshole. A real *mizera*.

Adopted after having been abused in foster care. How the hell was he supposed to know that? Though it did explain his opinions about Ben ending up in the hands of those who couldn't care less about him. Conor hadn't been speculating, he was speaking from experience.

Gunner had fucked this up, and it stopped now.

Headlights beamed through the dark, announcing Elias and Conor's return.

Gunner's stomach sank. What was he going to say? Sorry wasn't sufficient for what he'd done. How could he face Conor after this?

The singing hit him before he saw them. Was that Conor singing? When the two turned the corner, Elias led what had to be an intoxicated Conor toward the stairs. His arm was in a sling, and his wrist and hand were heavily bandaged.

"Why did you take him to get blitzed?" Gunner asked.

"I didn't. The doctor gave him pain medication, and it turns out our friend here is a lightweight," Elias explained while trying to keep Conor moving in the right direction.

"Hello. I'm back like that da-damn cat," Conor slurred. "I know he should've left me in town, but he wouldn't listen."

"Town?" Gunner quirked a brow.

"Yeah. He wanted me to drop him off at the motel," Elias said. "That was a hard *no* given his condition."

"Hey." Conor looked around wide-eyed. "It's dark."

"Yeah. That happens at night," Gunner stated.

"Cool. Have you noticed how many stars are out?" Conor stared up and stumbled a few feet away.

"Okay, up the stairs you go," Elias said while pulling the guy back onto the walkway and leading him forward.

Gunner jumped into the action, lifting Conor off the steps and safely depositing him onto the porch. But before he could get Conor through the garden doors, the guy sank into one of the patio chairs.

"This is nice," Conor said with a goofy smile.

Yep. He wasn't feeling any pain.

Elias moved to pick up Conor, but Gunner stepped in.

"It's okay. Leave him, and I'll make sure he gets up into bed."

Elias gave him a measured look. "You sure that's a good idea?"

"Listen, man. I'm not going to hurt the guy."

"More than you have already?" The sheriff's tone was strong. "He has every right to charge you with assault and battery."

"I only wanted to move him away from Julia." A criminal charge leveled against him when it seemed he'd have to fight to keep custody of Ben—he'd be fucked.

"Yet here we are." The sheriff wasn't budging.

Gunner respected Elias's law-and-order attitude, but now wasn't the time. He could understand Elias's concern, but he had to figure out a way to convince him he wasn't a threat.

"I tripped on the rug," Conor sing-songed off-key. "It wasn't Gunner's fault. I shouldn't've made Julia cry."

"Man, none of this is your fault," Gunner huffed. "I'm the idiot who's too afraid to accept your help." *Where did that come from?*

"Afraid of me? Have you ever looked in a mirror? You could squish me like a bug." Conor demonstrated by lifting the index finger of his right hand and pushing it against the chair's armrest with a little twist, all while maintaining a toothy smile.

"I don't mean physically," Gunner groaned and wiped the palm of his hand over his face.

"Ah, a breakthrough," Elias said while stretching out his arms. "Make sure he gets to bed safely."

"Got it."

With a nod, Elias left the two of them alone on the porch. Gunner sat and stared off into the darkness. *A breakthrough? What the hell did he mean by that?*

"So why are you 'fraid of little ol' me?" Conor's speech was slow and drawn out.

"How much pain medication did they give you?"

"Not enough," he said as he tried to raise his left arm, which was in a sling. "Still hurts."

Gunner quickly stopped him from reinjuring himself by softly pushing his arm down. "You gotta leave that arm down, okay?"

"Okay," Conor said as he slumped back into the chair like a petulant child. "Why don't you want my help?"

What was it about Conor's help that bothered him? "I don't know."

"It's free," Conor mumbled, making Gunner smile for the first time since he sat his ass out here waiting for Conor to return.

"It's not about the expense." Gunner had saved his money for a rainy day, and when his sister died, the monsoons hit. He'd never been so thankful for living a frugal life when the bills started coming in.

"My grandmother says accepting help is a sign of strength, not weakness," Conor said in an apparent moment of clarity before his drug-addled mind took over once again. "Or some flowery shit like that."

Gunner thought about that for a moment. Was he afraid to accept his help because he didn't want to appear weak? Why then could he accept the team's help without a problem? This brought up more questions than answers, and he wasn't willing to deal with that shit right now.

"Why didn't you mention you were adopted?"

Conor sat up straight, and his mouth hanging open. It would've been funny if the topic wasn't so important. "Julia told you?"

"Of course, she did. She was trying to explain why she was crying."

"Oh, yeah." Conor looked down at his busted wrist as if just remembering what'd happened. "That's okay then. She said she wouldn't keep my secret if someone could get hurt. I never thought it'd be me."

"You still haven't answered my question."

Conor turned his dopey eyes Gunner's way. "Can you repeat the question, teacher?"

"Okay, it's time to put you to bed," Gunner said. They'd have to have this discussion another time.

"But I want to stay up late and watch television." Conor stuck his bottom lip out and attempted to cross his arms, which ended in a yelp when he hit his wrist.

"You've had a big day. It's time for bed, *komarad*," Gunner played along. "Now stand up." He slid his hands under Conor's armpits and carefully lifted him until he was back on his feet.

"Do you remember where my bedroom is?" Conor asked.

"Yeah."

"Good, 'cause I don't." Conor laughed as they made it through the garden doors. "And what's with the Czech language bombs? Are they all swear words?"

"Not all, but most."

"Will you teach me some?"

"Czech swear words?" At Conor's nod, Gunner continued. "Sure. Whatever."

Gunner had Conor's right arm draped over his shoulders as he lifted the guy up the stairs to his bedroom. Conor began singing some god-awful tune as they made their way down the hallway.

"Shhh. People are sleeping. We have to be quiet."

Conor huffed, "You're no fun, are you?"

Gunner shook his head. "I'm plenty fun."

"When?"

"When I want to be."

"Will I ever see it?"

"Doubtful."

"I get it," he said as Gunner shuffled him into his bedroom. "You hate me."

For the love of God. "I don't hate you. I find you annoying."

Gunner lowered Conor onto his bed and knelt to remove his shoes.

"That's okay. I can be annoying," Conor admitted. "I'm not everyone's cup of…um."

"Tea."

"No, thank you. I don't like tea."

Gunner felt the lead in his stomach growing. How had he been so off about this guy?

"Well, I can be grumpy and stubborn," Gunner admitted.

"Yeah, you can." Conor smiled before leaning back against his pillows.

Gunner brought Conor's legs and feet up onto the bed and, for a moment, considered removing his jeans so he could get comfortable. But Gunner changed his mind when it appeared Conor was asleep. He raised up the covers and tossed them over him, then shut off the light and turned to leave.

He was almost out the door when Conor's sleepy voice whispered, "I promise to be good, ma'am, don't send me back there."

Gunner shut the door and rested his forehead against its worn surface.

Conor continued to mumble in his sleep, tearing at the shreds of Gunner's self-respect.

Tomorrow would be a new day, and he'd be a different man.

He'd prove he wasn't *that* asshole.

CHAPTER THREE

Conor

Conor woke up knowing he'd had surgery, and looked down at his casted hand and wrist through bleary eyes.

Yep, it hadn't been a dream.

He'd been pretty out of it the last few days due to the pain meds he'd been taking. Good stuff, but it made time waft weird, and made him fuzzy.

Now that the surgery had been done, he could begin healing, and he intended to cut back on the pain meds. He couldn't go around loopy for another week.

"You're awake," a nurse said as she came over to check on him. "How are you feeling?"

"Sleepy." Even though he'd only woken up.

"On a scale of one to ten, one being the lowest and ten being the highest, how's your pain?" she asked.

"About a four." Even though he was in a bit more pain than that, he could handle it.

"Hmm." She eyed him like she didn't believe him. "You rest. You'll be in recovery for a couple of hours."

"Okay. Thanks."

Conor settled in, expecting to fall right back to sleep, but his mind went in another direction. Straight to his favorite obsession. *Gunner*.

It felt as if they'd hit a turning point in their relationship. Whether that was due to their talk or Gunner's guilt for what he'd accidentally done, was still a mystery. But things had changed. The animosity was gone, and Gunner's protectiveness over Ben had seemed to lower, allowing Ben to come into Conor's room to visit and stay a while.

Conor understood Gunner's reaction that led to the broken wrist. He would've done the same thing in Gunner's shoes. Conor was the one who'd gotten twisted in the rug and fallen. It wasn't as if Gunner had thrown him across the room or anything equally dramatic.

Elias told Conor he could file assault charges against Gunner, which he immediately refused to do. It'd been an accident and nothing more.

Work on the cottages continued without him, for which he wasn't overly upset. The injury to his wrist would keep him out of any further construction projects for a couple of months. If there were a silver lining in all this, it would be no more hauling wood, and that he was right-handed. It was the left he'd broken. He also believed his broken bones saved him from passing out in front of the team with heat stroke. Win-win.

"Um, Mr. O'Brian," the nurse from earlier called as she rushed to his side. "There's a woman who refuses to wait until you're out of recovery—"

"Where is he?" a familiar voice asked.

You've got to be kidding me. "Grandma Jackie?"

Sure enough, she rounded the corner with the speed of a woman half her age, Aunt Viv in her wake. "Sweetheart. There you are."

"How? Who? When did you get here?" Conor asked, knowing he hadn't intended to call her until well after the surgery.

"Well, it wasn't as if you called me," Grandma Jackie groused as she adjusted his sheets.

"That was intentional. You're both crazy."

"Is that any way to treat your family?" She feigned indignation, but he knew better.

"You know I love you guys."

"Then why did we have to receive a call from a man we don't know to find out you broke your wrist?" Aunt Viv joined in the interrogation. *Great. Double-teaming me.*

The nurse looked stunned, but that was only the beginning. The curtain swished back again and in walked Gunner. Now it was a party. He looked shocked and a bit frazzled, which Conor found attractive. *What? No, no, no crushing on the big guy.*

"I left you two for sixty seconds to get your coffees. How the hell did you get in here?" Gunner asked while checking over Conor. "How do you feel?"

"You're all going to have to leave and return to the waiting room." Another nurse tried backing up the first.

It didn't work.

"Is this your fault?" Conor stared at Gunner, who looked as guilty as sin. "Thanks."

Grandma turned and wrapped her arm around Gunner's. "You be nice to this kind man. At least he had the decency to call us."

"I wanted to wait a bit to save you two the worry," Conor stated then glared at Gunner. "How the hell did you get their phone number?"

"Spence."

"Well, shit."

"Hello, I'm the hospital coordinator, Mr. Roades. I must ask you all to leave the recovery unit immediately or I'll be forced to call security. You're impeding the recovery of several patients." The man looked barely out of college and was wearing a sweater vest.

Conor had to admit, he wasn't feeling all that well. His wrist was throbbing, and his head had begun swimming.

"You have to go," he said. "I'll see you when I'm released from recovery."

"Are you sure you're okay?" Gunner asked.

"Promise. I'm good." He looked to Gunner. "Please take them back to the lake house," he said, needing a bit more peace before jumping into the fray of his constantly vocal, loving family. He adored them, but right now, he needed silence.

"Are you sure?" Grandma Jackie asked.

"I am. I need to rest right now," he assured them. "Thank you for being here."

"Oh, darling. I wouldn't be anywhere else," Grandma Jackie said as she brushed a piece of hair off his forehead.

"Love you guys."

"Love you too, now rest," she ordered as if it wasn't their fault he wasn't resting in the first place.

Mr. Roades ushered the three out of the recovery room, and Conor looked over at the first nurse who'd approached him when he opened his eyes.

"On second thought, I could use a top-up of meds, please."

She looked at him and nodded. "Understood."

***

Two days later

"They're taking over," Conor grumbled from his spot on the porch. "I love them and all, but I haven't lived with them in a long time. They can be overwhelming."

"At least someone is cooking while Rick and Roman are in Dallas," Julia said. "You don't want me cooking. I wouldn't even know where to start with all you guys and the amount of food you put away in a day."

"Gunner can cook," Conor suggested.

"He has enough to do with the construction and caring for Ben," Julia countered.

"Sophia would have loved this," Kyle said as he adjusted his walker away from the railing. "From what I've been told, she was a spitfire."

Fletch's younger brother sat with them while Shaw and Bryan helped with the construction. The three lived on a ranch outside of Marshall, and Shaw was part of the former SEAL team.

"I like them. Makes the place seem homier somehow," Julia stated as the team continued with the builds. The symphony of hammers, saws, and eighties and nineties rock belting out on the radio continued from sunup to sundown.

"They won't leave until I'm healed."

"So, six weeks isn't that long," Kyle said.

"There you are, darling," Grandma said as she walked out of the garden doors and onto the porch. "Your Uncle Marty called to say it's done."

Shit. That wasn't public knowledge.

"Who's Uncle Marty?" Julia asked.

Before Conor could say a word, Grandma continued. "Aunt Viv's brother runs the largest private investigations company on the East Coast. Conor followed in his footsteps."

"Do I want to know what 'it's done' means?" Julia asked.

Again, Grandma spoke up before Conor could open his mouth. "Conor asked Marty to spread the word about those nasty people he got swindled by to follow Gunner around."

"What does spread the word mean?" Gunner asked, making Conor jump.

"You need to wear a damn bell," Conor growled.

"It means no other PI in the area will accept jobs from those people, and if they do, they'd have to answer to the licensing board." Grandma was chock-full of information. He had to stop this before she and Aunt Viv got completely out of hand.

Conor glanced around at the shocked expressions. "What? Don't you think PIs have ethics?" Did they all see him as a lowlife?

Gunner shook his head with another one of those undecipherable expressions on his face.

"Not only that—" Grandma began, but Conor quickly cut her off.

"No. That's all."

Grandma nodded. "Yes, that's all concerning this case."

"I'm not buying it," Gunner stated. "But I respect your privacy and trust it's nothing that'll harm my family."

"You can trust that's of the utmost importance," Conor assured, hoping that would be the end of the subject.

Letting Gunner in on any of Conor's plans could read disaster, especially if they failed. He'd already disappointed Gunner enough.

"Okay."

"Okay?"

"Yeah, okay. I'm trusting you," Gunner stated.

Conor let out a whoosh of breath. "Well, thanks."

As Gunner started to walk toward the construction site, he asked Grandma, "Can I take another pitcher of that sweet tea you make out to the guys?"

"Of course, dear," she said as she placed her arm around Gunner's, turning him back to the house.

"Okay, what gives?" Julia asked.

"Let's say I'm looking into something that might help Gunner's case. I'm going on a hunch."

"The court date is only a couple of months away," Kyle reminded everyone.

"That's why I need help from my uncle. He has ways of finding things."

"You're a puzzle, Conor O'Brien," Kyle said with a smile. "I think you're good for him."

"Good for who?"

"Gunner," Julia said at the same time as Kyle.

"Wait a minute. There is no Gunner and me. I'm doing this because I feel like shit for having taken a case I shouldn't have, which could've hurt Ben. I have to right the situation. That's all."

"Okay," Julia said with a cheeky smile.

"Seriously, nothing is going on between us."

"Whatever you say," Julia agreed, but he could tell she didn't mean it. "Let's table that discussion for later. I have something else much more interesting for us to do."

"That doesn't sound creepy at all," Conor said while eyeing her suspiciously.

"Come on. I'll show you," she said before standing and walking into the lake house.

Kyle looked at Conor. "After you."

"Gee, thanks."

Conor stood and waited for Kyle to stand in case he needed help with his walker. He opened the door and held it for Kyle.

"Hey, you first." Kyle laughed, refusing to go through.

"I'm okay here, and I'm holding the door for you like I was raised to do." Conor laughed.

"Yeah, sure you are." Kyle grinned and went inside.

Considering he didn't hear any screaming, Conor went inside to find Julia pulling old bankers boxes out from one of the closets. He rushed over to help, only to realize he couldn't pick up anything with his busted wrist.

"It's okay," Julia said. "They're not as heavy as carrying around my Matthew."

Conor had to agree. Carrying a five-year-old was a workout.

"What do you have there?"

"As we cleaned the lake house, we came across boxes of paper and notes. I started storing them here, hoping to look at them someday and maybe figure out what they are."

"Today's that day?" Conor asked.

"Why not? Since we have Brick's permission, we can finally go through these and dump what's not important," Julia said.

Silence.

"Oh, come on, guys. It's not all that bad. You can sit in an air-conditioned kitchen and piece together a mystery."

"Mystery?" That got Conor's attention.

"Yep. From what I've read, it involves several families in this county. Are you game?"

Conor couldn't help himself when it came to investigating a mystery. "I'm in."

"So am I. What else do we have to do while the guys are outside working on the cottages," Kyle said.

"You do remember you run a business," Julia said to Kyle.

"Yeah, but it's managed so well I have hardly anything to do," Kyle said. "And a mystery sounds like so much fun."

"Yay," Julia cheered.

"First, we should organize the information by date, if they have any," Conor suggested.

"Good idea," Gunner said as he walked past with a large pitcher of sweet tea.

"I do have them on occasion," Conor replied.

"I know." Gunner laughed and continued walking out the door.

Conor couldn't help but watch him go.

"Yeah. Sure. Nothing's going on." Julia chuckled under her breath.

CHAPTER FOUR

Gunner

The floor creaked under Gunner's weight as he attempted to sneak out of Ben's room after his nephew had fallen asleep during their bedtime story. Gunner looked over his shoulder, thankful his nephew remained fast asleep. He double-checked the night-light, and then softly closed the door.

On his way down the stairs, he couldn't help thinking about how Conor always said he needed to wear a bell. As if thinking of him conjured him, Gunner walked into the living to see Conor sitting on the sectional with one of the old boxes on the floor beside him.

"You still at it?" Gunner asked as he watched the guy flatten a small piece of paper on his knee with his one good hand. "Where's Jackie and Viv?"

"My grandma and aunt have headed to their bedroom." They were sharing the large suite downstairs that used to be Kyle's. "And yeah. I'm still at it. It's addictive, and now I know why Julia couldn't let it go."

"Really? What've you found so far?"

"Some priest shot a dude. I found from this newspaper clipping. There are comments about a trial."

"Hmm. What year was that?"

"I haven't been able to find a piece with a date on it, but by the look of their clothing in the picture, it has to be in the early 1960s."

"That's interesting, but not really a mystery."

"Not unless he didn't do it."

"What makes you say that?"

"No one placed the priest at the site of the shooting, and it wasn't until the next day that he came forward and confessed."

"Or he could have run away after he did the deed and come to his senses the next day."

"Also true. We'll never know unless we keep digging." Conor wiggled his eyebrows, and Gunner smiled.

"Is it all about this priest?" This number of boxes couldn't be all about a murdering priest.

"No, there are land surveys and letters between two people, but it only shows their initials."

"Curiouser and curiouser."

"Indeed, Cheshire cat," Conor said with a laugh, and it took Gunner a few seconds to figure out the reference.

"Alice in Wonderland."

Conor grinned, and Gunner couldn't hold back his smile. That'd been happening a lot lately. Now that he wasn't trying to pick the man apart, Gunner found him interesting, which was odd because he didn't find many people interesting. Annoying, stressful, and selfish, but not interesting.

"Do you want any help?" The words were out of his mouth before he realized he was going to say anything. "If that's okay."

"Of course, it is. I'd love the help. But aren't you tired from all the construction stuff you've done today in the hot sun?"

"I've still got some energy left. How do you want them sorted?"

"I'm trying to divide them into decades. Then, if I can break them down by years, that'll help us get to the bottom of whatever this is."

"I can do that," Gunner said before digging into the box and retrieving a pile of dry, brittle, often yellowed paper.

The two sat quietly, sorting through what appeared to be a history of Marshall, or at least a snapshot of a time and event that took place in in the town. The silence was broken up by the occasional "look at this," or "what do you think this is."

Before he knew it, Sophia's antique wall clock sounded twelve gongs.

"It's getting late," Conor said. "We should probably hit the hay." Then he quickly followed that up. "I mean, go to bed. Not together. But go to bed separately, you know, to our rooms. Separate."

Gunner couldn't help but chuckle. "I know what you meant, and I agree. There's lots to do tomorrow, and we need some rest."

"Exactly," Conor said as he let out a breath and stood. "Thanks for your help. Good night, Gunner."

"Good night, Conor."

Gunner sat alone on the couch for a while, thinking about the mess coming his way in a couple of months. Brick and Roman had arranged for a lawyer, as they were more clued in on how to get the right one for the job.

Actually, Roman was more clued in, but Brick put his seal of approval on it. The attorney they found had a great reputation for winning custody hearings, which was exactly what Gunner needed.

He'd had a meeting with the attorney, Ms. Ruiz, and he had a good feeling about her fighting as hard as she could to keep Ben with Gunner. They'd filed their response, and now all that was left was the waiting. The worst part.

Knowing Conor had talked to his uncle to ensure no other PI showed up at their doorstep allowed Gunner to breathe a bit easier and stop looking over his shoulder. Tomorrow was the day he had to fill in Ben on what was happening because the little guy would have to be interviewed by a state child psychologist to determine if Ben was suffering being with Gunner as the in-laws had accused.

How was he going to explain to a kid that after losing his mom, he might lose his uncle and be forced to live with strangers? Who in their right mind would do that to a five-year-old? He could feel his anger building at what those people were forcing him to do. It was complete bullshit.

They'd never set eyes on the boy, and had never sent Ben a birthday card or Christmas present. Before now, they behaved as if he didn't exist, and suddenly they wanted to be stellar grandparents. That had to count for something. Their lack of interest in their grandchild, a kid whose father had relinquished all parental rights, had to tell the judge they didn't want Ben as much as they didn't want Ben being raised by a gay man.

Spence had dug into the grandparents' background and found nothing useful. They belonged to the right country club, hobnobbed with the right people, and even had a wing of a large university library named after the family. While they sounded upstanding on paper, they'd abandoned their grandchild for five years. If Gunner wasn't gay, they wouldn't've given Ben a second thought.

This whole situation sucked, and for the first time in his adult life, Gunner had no control over the situation. There was nothing he could do to change the state of play. This was new battleground his training had never prepared him for.

Sis, I could use your advice right about now.

***

Conor

Conor closed his bedroom door and stopped to lean his back against it. What was wrong with him? He had to be out of his mind to think what he was thinking. It could never be. Ever. But here he was daydreaming about it.

Gunner went from barely tolerating his existence to being somewhat friendly. Hardly a ringing endorsement to cause Conor to lust after the guy. But he had to admit, he'd been off-kilter since taking on the job Lisa and Frank Wells, the horrible in-laws, had offered. Although he hated what he'd done, Conor couldn't help but wonder what it would've been like if he'd never met the team. Never met Gunner. Where would he be now. He looked down at his cast and thought, *well, I probably wouldn't've had to have surgery for a broken wrist,*

One thing he knew for sure: if he hadn't taken the job, another PI would have. Not that it did anything to assuage his guilt. When he'd promised to make it up to Gunner, Conor meant it. First by contacting his uncle to ensure Gunner wasn't harassed anymore, and second by doing some research himself.

He'd called in several favors for one bit of information, hoping it panned out. If not, he'd have to rely on the justice system to do the right thing. But that was not always a given.

Conor would do whatever it took to ensure Ben wasn't forced to be with people he didn't know or want. He understood better than most, having lived the hell of being in a house where no one gave a shit about him. Ben, a sweet little kid who'd already lost enough, had to be protected at all costs. He had to stay with his Uncle Gunner.

Conor had been drawn into this mess under false pretenses, but his emotions were real. For the boy and for Gunner. He'd see this through and do what he came here to do and leave once it was over.

Damn that sounded so empty and unsatisfying. But he knew better than to wish for something he could never have. So, he'd keep his promise to protect Ben. Whatever else was percolating in his subconscious would burn out over time. Nothing could and would ever happen between him and the grumpy SEAL.

On to more mysterious endeavors like the over-fifty-year-old case of the priest and a shooting. Brick's great-aunt Sophia had kept these boxes for a reason, and Conor wanted to uncover what that was. The bug had bitten him as bad as it had Julia, and he was sure Kyle would be back to do some more digging.

Of course, it could be a wild-goose chase, but Conor didn't feel like it was. He'd seen file folders in a couple of boxes with official-looking documents. But adhering to his system prevented him from skipping over to another box while he was still halfway through the first. The investigation had to be methodical to avoid missing something along the way.

He couldn't help but wonder what would drive a priest to kill someone. Father Henry Jones had been in Marshall a little over a year when the shooting happened. His parishioners had voiced disbelief when the news broke. Still, with his signed confession, the DA went forward with a trial where the priest was found guilty and was sentenced to life without the possibility of parole.

Tomorrow, Conor was going to put out a few feelers and make a few calls about the whereabouts of Father Henry Jones. He'd been twenty-two in nineteen sixty-nine, the year he was sentenced, so there was a chance the man was still alive.

Conor stripped out of his clothes and got ready for bed. Normally, he slept in a pair of shorts, but tonight he decided to forgo them before crawling under the covers. Turning off his light did nothing to dim the full moon outside his window, as its glow made the room an ethereal chamber.

He rolled onto his back and stared up at the freshly painted ceiling. Repairs and renovations had been moving along nicely. He'd seen a few pictures of the state of the house when Brick had moved in, and the difference was astounding. They'd been able to work on it between missions, but two years later, they'd done so much.

The kitchen was enlarged and modernized as they waited on the new appliances and flooring to finish it up. The four upstairs bedrooms had been torn down to the studs and rebuilt. The three downstairs bedrooms were in various states of repair, with his grams and aunt staying in the most complete suites with their own bathroom. The living room had new hardwood floors, and the woodburning fireplace had been converted to a gas fireplace.

The roof had been replaced, the porches had been rebuilt, the house repainted, and a brand-new storm cellar had been installed. Gunner had shown him where it was in case the weather got bad. Apparently, they'd already been through a few severe storms.

Heavy footsteps passed outside his door, and Conor guessed Gunner was heading to his bedroom, which was right beside his nephew's. Ben has been adamant about staying close to his uncle, and who could blame the kid after losing his mom. They'd set up the rooms to have an adjoining door. That way, Ben could get to Gunner quickly, and vice versa.

Conor wondered what would happen when they moved into their cottage, which would have two separate bedrooms. Would Ben be ready to sleep without the connecting door? Conor doubted he'd still be around when the cottages were completed, so he'd never know.

He heard the water turn on in the closest of the two upstairs bathrooms. *Fuck.* Gunner was taking a shower. Now how was Conor supposed to fall asleep when his imagination was running rampant with images of a naked Gunner slicked wet. A naked Gunner soaped up. Conor soaping up a naked Gunner.

Visions of that tatted, ripped body covered in sudsy water, trails of bubbles funneling down between his hard pecs and cascading over those tight abs. His strong shoulders and biceps scrubbing every inch clean.

Holy fucking shit.

Conor's mind wasn't the only part of his body paying attention to what was going on in the bathroom less than fifteen feet away. His single-minded dick was getting painfully hard with every passing moment.

He tried to erase the images his brain had conjured and forced himself think of something that was completely unrelated to straddling those thick, muscular thighs. Then he heard what sounded like a bar of soap drop onto the tiles and pictured those toned ass cheeks sticking up in the air.

He had no other choice. He reached down and took himself in hand. There was no way he'd fall asleep unless he dealt with the lust throbbing through his veins. He pumped his hand up and down his rock-hard dick, using the pad of his thumb to spread the drops of precum over the sensitive head.

With every thrust, the images in his mind became more erotic: he was in the shower with Gunner in all manner of pleasurable positions.

Then he heard it.

A soft moan reverberating from the shower.

Barely audible, but considering he was fixated on what was going on in the bathroom, Conor caught it.

Was Gunner doing the same thing? Were they jacking off at the same time?

Another moan.

Fuck yeah, he was.

Conor felt the warning tingles and increased his hand speed until he grabbed a pillow and groaned his release into memory foam.

He had the stray thought that the pillow would remember this and hoped it had no ability to communicate the retained memory.

A few minutes later, the water stopped and eventually the bathroom door opened.

Gunner was returning to his room.

Conor couldn't help but wonder who the big guy was thinking about while doing himself.

It didn't matter.

It wasn't Conor, and it would never be.

CHAPTER FIVE

Gunner

"You don't want me anymore?"

The words cut like a knife straight through Gunner's chest before burying deep in his heart.

"No, no. That's not true. I'll always want you."

"Then why am I going away?"

"You're not going anywhere if I can stop it."

"I don't understand, Uncle Gunner." Tears streamed down the little boy's red cheeks.

"Neither do I, buddy. But I'm going to fight to keep you right here. Is that okay with you?"

Ben jumped up from his seat on the patio chair and ran into Gunner's open arms. "I want to stay with you," he howled.

"Then that's what we'll fight to do. No one is going to take you away from me. Never ever, ever."

Gunner pulled Ben onto his lap and wrapped his arms around the little guy. The two sat staring at the lake for a long time as fear and anger warred for supremacy in Gunner's mind. Fear of losing Ben and anger at having been forced to scare his young nephew like this. He wished he could make it all go away, but he had no idea how to accomplish that. He wasn't allowed to make a threat in the civilian world as easily as he could on a battlefield.

Being blessed with perfect vision, nerves of steel, and a steady hand had made Gunner the perfect candidate for sniper training. His ability to hit his mark over ninety-eight percent of the time in all possible conditions, and while coming under fire, had served him well over the years, but it did absolutely nothing for him now.

He felt hollow and powerless. Two things that didn't track with his personality or his life creed. There was no one to fight physically, no mission to complete. This was his and his nephew's life being messed with, and it made him crazy he couldn't just stop it.

What if the judge decided he wasn't a suitable person to raise Ben? What would he do? His first thought was to take Ben and disappear. With his friends, that wasn't out of the realm of possibilities. New names, new histories, and maybe even a new country. Canada wasn't so far away.

The bigger question was, could he do that to Ben? Pick up and leave everything he knew again? However, the same would happen if the in-laws won the court case. His mind was being torn into what felt like a million different directions, and no matter what he tried, he couldn't re-center himself like he'd done hundreds of times waiting to hit his targets.

Gunner looked away from the lake at the sound of his nephew's small snore. Sure enough, when he looked down, Ben had cried himself to sleep in Gunner's arms. It hurt him knowing that at his nephew's tender young age, he already knew unbearable pain and loss, and this situation added fuel to the embers of a fire that would never be put out. Ben would always miss his mother.

The screen door opened with a soft squeak, and Gunner turned to find Conor holding one of Ben's favorite blankets.

"I thought this might help," he whispered before walking close and laying it on top of Ben.

"Thank you."

"Would you prefer to be alone?"

"No." He was already in his mind enough. Sitting alone while Ben slept soundly only intensified the feeling.

Conor took a seat in a patio chair a couple of feet away. "How is he?"

"Confused and scared."

"Yeah, I get that, but this fight is far from over."

"I told him I'd fight to keep him right here."

"We'll fight to keep him right here," Conor corrected.

Gunner looked Conor straight in the eye and could see the conviction in those pale blue depths.

With a nod, he said, "We."

Conor's smile was instant, and for the first time Gunner really understood how committed the guy was to protecting Ben. You couldn't fake it this well, and the pros had taught Gunner how to read people. He had to admit he'd been way off base about the guy's true intentions.

"Thank you," Gunner mumbled. Emotions were foreign to him after years of turning that part of himself off to do his job effectively. "For helping us."

"I always keep my word," Conor said softly.

"No. It's more than that. You owe me nothing, yet you're using your contacts to protect Ben. Hell, you threw yourself over me when I went down in that storage facility, and I repaid you with a broken wrist."

"Couldn't let Ben lose another loved one. And for the ten millionth time, my wrist is not your fault. My feet got tangled in the rug. I shouldn't've thrown my arm out like I did to slow the impact. It was an accident. When are you going to accept that?"

"Are you always this easy to get along with?"

"Hell no. You're just lucky." Conor chuckled.

"I don't know about luck."

"Ooo, burn. And here I thought we were bonding."

"Bonding." Gunner laughed softly, so as not to wake Ben. "I never thought that word would be used in the same sentence as us, but miracles happen."

"Ah, you're sweet. I've never been called a miracle before." Conor pretended to fluff his short hair. "It's about time someone noticed."

And just like that, Gunner felt measurably better.

"Not you. Don't be a *blbec*."

"*Blbec*?"

"Yeah. Moron, idiot."

"I'll have to remember that."

"You worried about being called an idiot?"

"Only around you."

"Fair enough."

Conor chuckled again, and Gunner found he liked the sound. Maybe there was more to the guy than he'd given him credit for. The operative word was *maybe*. He was more of a wait-and-see kind of person. Better to be late to the party than have to jump off the bandwagon when it all went south.

***

Conor

Hours later, Conor still couldn't get the conversation he'd had with Gunner out of his head. The longer he was at the lake house, the compelling, confusing man was taking up more and more of Conor's head space.

Even now, when he was knee deep in paper, he couldn't get his head straight. What the hell was wrong with him? He let out a long sigh and buried his head in his hands. He still had the cast on, but after the first few weeks, his arm became less pained and more mobile. Another six weeks to go, and he'd finally have it off.

"You okay?"

Conor turned to find Kyle watching him. He'd been lost in his thoughts, and for a split second forgot he wasn't alone.

"Yeah, I'm good. Nothing to worry about," Conor said as he straightened and grabbed another stack of envelopes from the box he was sorting.

"Nope, not buying it." Kyle scanned the kitchen and living room. "No one's here, and I swear to keep what you say under lock and key." The guy was a saint who'd been dealt a shitty hand by none other than his psychotic parents.

"It's nothing. Stupid stuff, especially considering all the shit going on around here." No way did this compare with the chance of losing Ben, or what Kyle had been through. Lined up against real problems, Conor's issues seemed trivial and selfish.

Kyle continued to stare at him. Clearly, he wasn't letting it go.

"Fine. You'll think I'm off my rocker anyway," Conor said as he double-checked his grandma or aunt weren't hiding around some corner trying to get the scoop. It wasn't only the men in his family that were PIs.

"You've got a boner for Gunner and don't know what to do about it?" For someone who acted like he didn't know what Conor was thinking, Kyle summed up quite efficiently.

Conor sat there with his mouth hanging open for a few moments. "Okay, freaky intuitive, man. What do I do about it?"

"Nothing. You do what you came here to do and leave." Kyle dug back into the box as if the discussion was over.

"Well, that wasn't what I expected you, of all people, to say." Kyle was the guy who followed his heart. And he had two men at home to prove it.

"But it's what you're going to do, right?"

"Probably."

"Never took you for a coward."

"I'm not a coward."

"Sure you are."

"Besides, he doesn't even like me."

"I wouldn't be so sure about that."

"Why? What have you heard?" Conor asked as he dropped the envelopes back into the box. "Did he say something?"

Kyle's wide smile was the first clue Conor had given himself away.

"Good to know my romance-o-meter's still working strong," Kyle teased, patting himself on the back.

"Funny, man. You're full of jokes." Conor rolled his eyes and hung his head. "It sucks when the person you're attracted to hates you."

"Hate's a strong word."

"But applicable considering I was the one who directed the in-laws where to serve him with the court papers."

"You carry a lot of guilt around, don't you?"

"Can't fight the truth."

"Sorta reminds me about how Gunner feels about your wrist there."

Conor looked down at his cast. "That's different."

"How?"

"I meant to find Gunner for the client. Gunner didn't intend to break my wrist."

"So it's intent, is it?"

"Makes all the difference in the world."

"Like murder and manslaughter? Very black and white in your world."

"It is. But, of course, there are areas of gray."

"Just not for you."

"Quit turning this around."

"How am I turning it around when it began with you and your frustration?"

"I don't know." Conor huffed and slumped back in his chair. "I'm screwed."

"Or at least you're trying to get screwed."

"Is that supposed to be helpful?"

"Yup. Do you see how silly all of this is? Second-guessing, guilt, and frustration get you nowhere. I should know. I carried around the guilt of my parents' deeds."

"You had nothing to do with any of that shit. You were the one who stopped the human trafficking."

"I lived with my parents for years, unaware of the evil they were doing. How was I so blind?"

"You weren't blind. You saved all those people as soon as you had enough evidence. You saved several young people in your neighborhood, not to mention the many more who would've been put in the pipeline."

"So, you're saying though I was smack-dab in the middle of the situation, the fact that I didn't know what was truly happening is some sort of free pass?"

"I wouldn't call it a free pass, but I would say it absolves you of any guilt."

"Hmmm, now, if I accept that point of view—"

"Like you should."

"Like I should, then explain to me why you're doing the same." Before Conor could respond, Kyle carried on. "You were in a situation but didn't know all the facts, and, like me, have been trying to make up for it ever since."

Conor sat dumbfounded. His brain was spinning like a top. True, he'd never looked at it that way and wondered if it was the same. According to Kyle, Conor shouldn't carry around the guilt of doing his job and he should forgive himself for getting suckered in by the in-laws.

As he thought it over, the garden doors flung open, and Julia ran inside.

"Ben's missing."

CHAPTER SIX

Conor

Fear like nothing he'd ever felt before blew over him like a whoosh of flames. Ben was missing.

Gunner and Fletch were in town picking up another load of lumber, but were racing back. Leaving Brick, Conor, Shaw, and Spencer to do the searching while Kyle, Julia, Matthew, and Grandma and Aunt Viv stayed behind in case Ben returned.

"When was the last time anyone saw him?" Brick asked the assembled group.

"He was playing by the side porch with Matthew last I saw him," Spence stated.

"That's right. They both came in for lunch," Julia said. "I thought Ben went up to his room after he ate. He's been out of sorts all day since Gunner had 'the' talk with him."

"Poor little man," Shaw said.

"When I went upstairs later, I couldn't find him. Then we went outside to look, and still nothing." Julia pulled her young son close.

"Okay, we'll spread out and check the forest. Spence, you take the waterfront while the three of us split up into the trees. If you find him, call or text your location."

"Got it," Conor said as he grabbed a first-aid kit and flashlight before the men split up.

He took the area Brick had pointed out and walked into the maze of trees without hesitation. Thanks to the recent installation of a satellite tower, their cell service was never in question, so he pulled out his phone and put the compass on the screen. His only thought was to find Ben and bring him home safely.

The deeper he went into the forest, the darker it got. Old-growth trees had created a canopy of branches and leaves, making visibility tricky.

"Ben. Ben," he yelled. "Can you hear me?"

Nothing. Conor carried on. He didn't race. He took his time methodically checking every hollow in the trees, looking behind rocks, and anywhere else a five-year-old could hide away from the world. The poor little guy had more than his share of pain and sadness in his short life.

Conor remembered the times he spent as a child wishing he could disappear, and he could understand Ben's reasoning. The way a child thought when confronted with going somewhere he didn't want to be was to run away.

At odd times he could hear the others calling out Ben's name, but the forest was large and sound seemed to bend around tree trunks even though there was a lot of space between each of the men. More than enough to guarantee they weren't tripping over each other.

It was already late afternoon, which didn't give them much time before dark, and they'd been at it for over an hour. Conor refused to give up. He continued to methodically check in every nook and cranny.

As the sun lowered, the branches took on a more menacing appearance. The shadows were long on the ground, and the air cooled slightly. They'd have to find him fast, or this would turn into a nighttime search, and it would mean Ben would be even more terrified out here all alone.

"Ben. Can you hear me?"

Nothing.

Come on, kid, give me a sign, please.

Then it happened. He heard something move slightly by a small indentation in the ground. As he got closer, more sounds became identifiable. Crying.

"Ben," he said. "It's Conor. I'm here to take you back to the house, buddy."

When Conor saw Ben, the relief brought him to his knees beside the young boy.

"Are you hurt?"

Ben shook his head but refused to look at him. Conor didn't like that.

He took a quick moment to text he'd found Ben before continuing his examination.

"Does anything need a Band-Aid?" He smiled while wiggling the small first-aid kit in front of Ben. "I think there are Spider-Man ones in here."

Ben finally looked up as Conor had hoped, and other than a bit of dirt and tearstains, he looked no worse for the wear. Conor could finally breathe a bit easier.

He held out his hand, which, thankfully, Ben took hold of immediately. "Your uncle is going to be so happy to see you."

"Why?" Ben mumbled under his breath.

That struck him as odd, but okay, he could roll with it. "He was scared when we couldn't find you."

"I'm going away soon anyway."

Now, this was an area of emotion Conor understood. He'd been through it countless times himself. The waiting for the social worker to pick him up and move him on to the next house never got better.

"I know it sucks, but I assure you you're not going anywhere."

"You don't know that." Ben had him on that one.

"You're right. I can't predict the future," he said as he and Ben sat down on a fallen log. He knew the team would be following his cell signal and arrive soon. He took out a bottle of water and handed it to Ben. "Drink up. You have to be thirsty."

"Okay."

"I may not be able to see what's going to happen tomorrow, but I have some valuable information. I know your uncle has and will do everything he can to keep you with him. I know everyone here at the lake house is doing the same. You know how big and strong all these guys are."

Ben nodded, and his tears stopped. That was a good sign.

"Well, knowing all that, you have to understand that no one or nothing will make you do something you don't want to do."

"Are you sure?"

"Positive. When I was a kid your age, I would've given anything to have this team on my side. They aren't going to let anything bad happen to you."

"Even you?"

"Absolutely. I'm here to make sure of it."

Ben looked at him for a few moments before jumping into Conor's arms. "I don't want to leave Uncle Gunner."

"Then that's what we'll make sure happens."

Conor knew they were no longer alone and looked up to find Gunner standing several feet away. The anguish on his face almost broke Conor, and instantly he lifted Ben and carried him over to his uncle.

"He's okay. Not a mark on him."

"Thank you for finding him."

Gunner reached for Ben, who flung himself into his uncle's waiting arms. "I'm sorry, I ran away."

"Promise me you'll never do it again."

"I promise."

Conor took that as his cue to leave, but when he turned, Gunner grabbed onto his arm. "Where you think you're going?"

"Um…"

"Uncle Conor told me you would never let me go, and I feel better now."

"He did, did he."

"Yeah. I'm hungry. Can we go home?"

"Sure, buddy. Let's get you cleaned up and fed. You've had a big day."

Ben nodded and laid his head on his uncle's broad shoulder. Conor figured the little guy would be asleep before they got out of the forest. He'd worn himself out.

Conor was happy he could help in some way.

***

Gunner

His hands were still shaking as they walked through the trees. And his hands *never* shook.

"He's asleep," Conor whispered. "Did the rest of the team head back to the house?"

"Yeah," was all he could manage while his body fought all his attempts at calming himself down.

Conor reached over and placed his hand on Gunner's arm. "He's safe. Everything will be okay. I promise."

Gunner felt warmth fill him. It was strange but welcomed at the same time. He'd always been the one to give protection and fix the problem. It'd been his job and his life as far back as he cared to remember. Now, for the first time, he needed someone else's strength, and shockingly it didn't come from his team, but from this man who wouldn't go away no matter how much Gunner had tried to get rid of him.

He caught himself thinking of Conor as more than the PI who got this whole shit show going. More than simply a friend.

This was dangerous territory, and he reacted with anger as he did whenever he faced change.

Gunner pulled back his arm and said, "I don't need your comforting. Everything's under control."

Conor's hand fell to his side, and before the guy could look away, Gunner registered the hurt in his expression.

"Understood," Conor said before taking the lead on their trek out of the forest.

He never looked back.

CHAPTER SEVEN

Conor

Conor sat in his room reading over the text he'd received from his Uncle Marty, who was on the East Coast where it was nearly four in the morning.

The Wellses are a piece of work. They've approached multiple agencies trying to dig up dirt on your friends. No one's biting. As for the other matter, it's not looking good. I'm sorry.

Thanks, Uncle Marty. I appreciate what you and everyone are doing.

Of course, kid. We're family.

Conor's mood lifted slightly at his uncle's words. It didn't matter a lick that he wasn't blood to them. His family was loyal.

I need this to be treated like family. We have no choice but to contact the Don and make a deal for his help.

You're that invested? This is no small act. Are you positive?

Conor thought about Ben and Gunner and how upset the boy was, and that look of anguish in Gunner's eyes when they were in the forest. Conor couldn't imagine what would happen if Ben was taken from Gunner permanently. The big guy may not share the same feelings as Conor, but that wasn't the barometer for him to do the right thing.

Conor typed the words, knowing the implications of what he was doing.

Yes. You and I both know he travels in circles we can't access.

Your grandmother isn't going to be pleased, but I'll do it. I'll contact the Don.

As soon as he read the words, Conor took a deep breath to center himself.

Thanks, Uncle Marty.

I hope your friend is worth it.

No child deserves what Ben has been through.

I meant the guy. I'd come guns blazing for the kid.

I know you would. The guy isn't involved in this.

What? Is he an idiot? You're a great catch.

Hahaha.

Conor set his phone on his bed and stared at the ceiling. They were running out of time. Ben was scheduled to meet with the social worker in four days, and then they were off to see the judge assigned to the case five weeks later.

He needed the information, and he needed it now if they were to keep Ben where he needed to be. Consequences be damned. It wasn't as if he couldn't do a little dirty work in order to get what he needed. He knew as soon as his uncle made contact with the Don, Conor was making a deal with the devil. *C'est la vie.*

He was pulled out of his thoughts by a single knock on his bedroom door. He looked over at his clock and wondered who would need him at two in the morning.

"Come in," he said as he stood. Thankfully he had his shorts on.

When the door opened, he couldn't have been more shocked.

"Gunner? Is something wrong?"

He hadn't heard any action going on downstairs or outside, but that meant nothing. These men worked in a world of silence, getting things done before anyone knew they were there and gone.

"No."

"Okay. So, what's up?"

He couldn't think of a reason for the big guy to be in his room. Gunner had made himself absolutely clear in the forest. So Conor had slammed that door shut, and bolted, welded, and barricaded it, and then tossed the key into the abyss. Okay, he might've been angry and hurt at the time, but needs must, and all that.

"We need to talk."

"You? Talk?"

"Funny guy, but yeah." He didn't sound pleased.

He shut the bedroom door and seemed nervous, which, for Gunner, was completely out of character.

"What's wrong?"

"Nothing. Everything. I don't fucking know," Gunner said as he ran his fingers through his dark hair.

"Sounds like you have a problem."

"You could say that."

He stepped aside, and with his arm out ushered Gunner into his room.

Conor couldn't send the dude away, especially after his earlier behavior. If Gunner needed help, Conor would help. It was the way he was wired. Which sucked sometimes.

"Okay, tell me all about it."

Gunner stared at him with an odd expression Conor had seen him use more and more often around him.

"What?" Conor asked.

"You're just going to invite me in and listen to me bitch?"

"Yeah. I thought that was obvious. Now, what's wrong?"

"Even after the way I treated you on the way back to the house?"

"Yeah, and thanks for reminding me. Now what the fuck is your problem?" Conor was a patient man, but Gunner was playing on his last nerve. It was late, he was tired, and now he was being forced to sit through whatever was pissing off the guy after Conor had been absolutely, one hundred percent rejected.

Fuck my life.

"This," Gunner growled before pushing Conor against the wall and taking his lips in a punishing, ravenous kiss that had him holding on to Gunner's shoulders for dear life.

The feel of Gunner's lips commanding his own set Conor on fire. His head swam with shock, and at the speed of how things had changed. But he had other ideas.

Conor took over the kiss and spun them around, placing Gunner against the wall. It was apparent the big guy wasn't used to men dominating him, but if this was going to happen, Gunner would have to learn he wasn't the only dominant male in the room.

To Conor's surprise, Gunner acquiesced, and Conor slowed the kiss to something more intimate and less brute force needy. That didn't mean he didn't like that, but here and now, he wanted to taste and explore the object of his desire.

Gunner's groan was music to his ears, and Conor wanted more. Their bodies molded together, and Gunner's hard bulge lined up with his own as excitement and desire rushed through his body.

As quickly as it started, it ended with Gunner's deep growl before he pushed Conor a couple of feet away.

Both of them were struggling to breathe, staring at each other with their chests heaving.

"What the hell was that?" Conor was the one growling now.

"The problem."

"Well, thank you very much, asshole. I'm sure you know the way out."

"*Sakra*. I didn't mean it to come out that way."

"*Sakra?*"

"Dammit."

"Oh. Then what way did you mean it?"

"I'm not good at this. Hell, give me a target at three thousand meters, and I'm good. But this shit's got me all screwed up, and I don't know which way is up. It's your fault."

"My fault? The last time I checked, you didn't want anything to do with me. How do you figure this is on me?"

"You could've been an asshole."

"Wait, you're pissed because I'm not an asshole? Are you sure you haven't been clubbed across the head one too many times while out on missions?"

Gunner began pacing. "I tried to ignore you and send you away. But no, you're here doing shit that makes me *feel*. Running around half naked driving me insane," Gunner said as he waved his hand in Conor's direction.

"This is my bedroom. I can be butt naked if I want to be."

Gunner stopped and gave Conor a long, heat-filled look from the top of his head to the soles of his feet. "Don't tempt me."

"Tempt you? I haven't done anything to tempt you. Why would I? You hate me, remember?"

"I remember."

"I don't know what's going on in that big head of yours, and at this moment I'm too tired and stressed to deal with your emotional awakening."

"Awakening? You make it sound like I'm traipsing through some damn flower garden. I'm bleeding out here, and you're making flower crowns or some shit."

"There's a picture."

"I'm in the middle of the battle of my life, trying to hold on to a kid who means more than the world to me, and I can't stop thinking about *you*. I'm working outside, you're there, taking a shower, and you're there. I close my eyes at night—"

"And I'm there. I get it. Then why did you get angry when I tried comforting you after we found Ben?" It was a fair question considering the guy's hot/cold behavior deserved an Oscar.

"It's how I deal with anything that changes the status quo," Gunner huffed.

"Status quo. Okay, you really don't like change, do you?"

"No."

"Is that why you didn't retire when the other team members did? You couldn't handle the change from your military life into civilian?"

"Yeah."

"Until your sister died, then you were forced to."

"Again, yeah."

"Okay, I'm starting to get a clearer picture of what's happening here."

"I'm glad one of us does."

"This is what we're going to do."

"What's that?"

"Nothing."

"Nothing? Seriously, that's all you've got? I'm a man of action. I don't do *nothing*."

"Well, get used to it because you've reminded me we have more important things to deal with than your inability to decipher your emotions."

Conor was done. Sure, he lusted after Gunner, but now that he'd sealed his fate to get the information he needed to assure Ben's future, a relationship with the man was no longer feasible. His mission was clear: he was meant to save Ben from a childhood filled with sorrow. Maybe he was meant to be here after all.

"Here I thought you gave a shit," Gunner grumbled.

"Don't even go there. I've dropped everything to help protect Ben. Hell, I would've surrendered my life that day in that firefight to ensure Ben didn't lose you. I've tried being nice to you and showing you how much I care, but I see that was a mistake. Obviously, this is the right time to table this emotion discussion. Our efforts are better served stopping your in-laws, not trying to make something work between us."

Gunner was quiet for a moment before speaking in a calmer tone. "That's the way you want it? Can you look at me straight and tell me you don't feel the same things I do?"

It would be so simple to say no. To say he didn't feel the same, but Conor couldn't pull it off as hard as he would've tried. "This has nothing to do with what I want. It's about what needs to be done. You don't need any more complications right now."

As he said the words, Conor realized how true they were. He'd kick himself in the ass if he could for even considering starting something with Gunner. This wasn't the time for any of that, and Conor was finally getting the message through to his fool heart.

The poor guy was being torn in so many directions, how the hell would Gunner be sure of his feelings? Attraction be damned.

"It's better this way, trust me. You'll thank me when you get all this courtroom business out of the way."

Gunner looked confused, and who could blame him. Until now, Conor hadn't considered the big picture, which had been selfish. He was disgusted with himself for ever considering starting something with a man who had lost his sister and was fighting to keep his nephew.

"I don't know what I expected, but this wasn't it," Gunner said.

"I'm sorry to be the voice of reason. It's not usually my thing. You're not in a good place right now, and starting something between us isn't going to help."

"Yeah, I get it." Gunner turned to leave.

"Believe me. It's not for lack of wanting." Conor needed to make that clear.

Gunner grinned. "We'll see."

CHAPTER EIGHT

Gunner

Gunner's shoulders were aching, but the pain was assuaged when he stood back and took in the beginnings of his and Ben's cottage. The first two walls were framed and up. They should have two more up before dark. The team had decided they'd concentrate on a pair of cottages at one time, and once the first two were ready, they'd move on to the next two until all seven were completed. Of course, that all had to happen between missions and assignments.

Gunner's and Ben's cottage was one of the first two, meaning they'd have their own space sooner rather than later. That was, of course, if the court case went his way. The date loomed like a specter over the entire lake house. Ben had already met with the assigned social worker, Hal Gentry, and everyone was interviewed, then Gentry did a comprehensive home inspection.

The meeting seemed to go well, but Gunner couldn't tell for sure until they learned, at the trial, what Gentry put in the report. Gunner's stomach rolled every time he allowed himself to think of life without Ben, and wasn't sure if he could do it. Certainly not now when he'd tasted what his life could be raising his sister's boy.

Gunner threw his hammer into one of the toolboxes and headed to the house to get a drink. He heard the singing before he neared the house. It sounded like one of the kids' television shows, only louder and filled with giggles.

Turning the corner to the back steps, he found Brick, Shaw, and Fletch standing on the porch looking through one of the side windows. Fletch shushed him before Gunner could ask what the hell was going on. Gunner stood beside them and looked inside the house. At what he saw, he pulled out his phone and hit record. There was no way he wasn't taping the full-on precious going on inside.

Ben and Mattie were dancing and singing using their new karaoke machine while Conor, Kyle, and Julia put on a show worthy of a planned, paid-for kids' party. Gunner had no idea where they found feathered boas or the matching rainbow-colored wigs, but whatever. The most important thing: they were having fun. After what Ben had been through these past couple of weeks, to see his boy laughing, singing, and dancing…that was all Gunner needed.

He kept recording, watching them with a smile on his face. Each had a microphone and sang to the song on the machine.

Kyle remained sitting while Conor and Julia danced around, whirling and twirling so fast it was dizzying. All five were laughing, and Ben was a carefree little boy having a great time with his family. Not a hint of worry or sadness as he sang and danced alongside Conor, and Gunner knew that was Conor's intent.

This was what Ben's childhood should be, fun and worry-free.

Then his mind went in a completely different direction as he focused on Conor's hips swaying and shaking to the beat of the music. Gunner was captivated. Conor had refused him, but he should've expected it after he'd treated the guy like an outsider and had been a real asshole.

Conor was right, though. Gunner could see now that he'd had time to think about the future. Now was not the time to make decisions about his personal life. All his energy had to go to Ben and keeping him here. Even knowing that, Conor continued to take up valuable time in Gunner's subconscious, and it wasn't easy to turn off the attraction.

He turned to look at Brick and Fletch, who were staring at him, not at what was going on in the house.

"What?"

"You were growling," Brick said.

"At least this time, it's got nothing to do with being angry." Gunner grinned before walking past them and into the lake house.

The moment the screen door closed behind him, all five "artists" stopped dancing and singing even though the karaoke machine kept playing the upbeat music. Then Conor shut it off.

"Gunner…um… Do you need something?" Julia asked.

"Nope, just enjoying the show." Gunner smiled, and Ben came running into his arms.

"Did you hear me singing?"

"Definitely. You've got some real talent."

Ben beamed and kissed Gunner on the cheek. Brick and Fletch came inside, and Conor did something unexpected.

"Two, three, four," he cheered and turned the music back on, to which all five began dancing and singing all over again.

The man was unashamed, and if Gunner wasn't wrong, he shook his hips with a bit more vigor. Gunner put Ben down so he could rejoin the party.

Julia whipped her pink boa around Mattie's shoulders and announced, "Dinner might be a bit late."

Conor and Ben shared a microphone and sang until they both broke out laughing. Gunner looked around the room at all the smiling, happy faces and couldn't imagine being anywhere else.

These people were his home and his heart. He didn't need time or space to come to that conclusion. All that was left was winning the custody hearing.

Then he had to convince the handsome man across the room that this *was* the right time to consider their future.

Gunner needed backup.

***

Conor

They were down to mere weeks before the trial, and Conor was a nervous wreck. He hadn't heard back from the Don, and his family still hadn't had any luck finding what he needed to stop all this bullshit dead in its tracks. At least he had a feeling what would stop it, but he worried he might be wrong.

"I can't believe all the information Sophia had collected about the priest and the murder case," Julia said from her pile of paper.

"There has to be a reason she kept it all," Conor surmised. "We're missing something."

Julia put her papers aside.

"Okay, here's what we got," Conor began. "A young and new priest to the community, Father Henry Jones, shot Mr. Jericho Miles, the local troublemaker. Jericho had been in jail on several occasions throughout his forty-five-year life. No one in the small community of thirteen hundred people saw who shot the guy. The next morning Father Henry Jones walks into the sheriff's station and confesses to the shooting."

"His confession was all the evidence they had," Julia said. "There was no weapon found or even a spot of blood on the priest, but they accepted his confession. It doesn't make sense to've had trial. He confessed. The DA should've taken the plea and that would've been the end of that."

"Yeah, well, there's more here. I'm sure of it. The priest refused to take the sheriff's advice and go home," Conor said, "which meant he didn't believe the priest did it."

"It seems clear no one was upset Jericho was dead," Kyle said. "His body wasn't claimed, and he was buried in one of the paupers' plots at the cemetery."

"Why would a priest kill the town miscreant?"

"I don't know," Spence said as he walked into the living room. "But, as you asked, I looked up Father Jones. He's alive and well in the Torres Unit of the state pen over in Hondo."

Conor appreciated Spence taking the time to find the priest. He'd been busy tracking down leads regarding the cover-up surrounding the missing children who'd been part of the Noah Project.

"He's alive?" Julia gasped.

"You know what that means?" Kyle stated. "Road trip."

"Best to go to the source to get some answers," Conor agreed. "How far away is it?"

He was an East Coast guy. Texas was a not a place he'd spent any time before coming to Fire Lake. Kyle pulled out his phone and went to work as Spence walked up to Conor.

"Got a minute?" Spence asked.

"Sure," Conor replied, curious what this could be about, and followed Spence into the other room.

"What's up?"

"I know what you're trying to do."

"And what's that?"

"I tried finding him as well."

Shit. "No luck, I'm guessing."

"None."

"That's what I was afraid of."

"Jason Wells is a ghost and wants to remain that way."

"I can't accept that. I have to find Ben's bio father. He's the only one who could make this whole thing disappear."

"How do you know that?"

"It's a gut feeling. Something isn't right in the Wells household, and I want to find out what that is."

"Does Gunner know?"

"No. There's no use in getting his hopes up if we can't find the guy."

"Jason signed away his parental rights."

"Yes, I'm aware, and it doesn't make sense. There's more to this than we know. I can feel it."

"Is that why you made a deal with Don Reza?"

"You're good." Conor was impressed Spence had sussed that out.

Spence grinned. "I know. That's why I'm warning you not to make a deal with the devil."

"Too late. He's got a long reach and access to people and places we don't. We only have weeks left before Gunner and Ben go before the judge. I did what I had to do."

With a narrow gaze, Spence scrutinized him top to toe. "We'll see."

He walked away, leaving Conor confused, wondering what was with these guys and the multiple uses for the term "we'll see." Gunner had said the same thing the other night when he told him now wasn't the time to start anything between them. It felt like the end wasn't the true end for these guys. Where normal people saw a wall, these guys saw opportunity.

Pffft. SEALs. Definitely a breed apart.

Conor walked back into the living room and sat down.

"That thing bugging you?" Julia asked.

"What?" Conor asked.

Julia pointed, and Conor realized he was scratching the skin under the edge of his cast.

"I can't wait for this thing to be removed. It's driving me up a wall." The itching was distracting and endless.

"Only a couple more weeks."

"Right. And it can't come soon enough."

"I got it," Kyle shouted.

"What?" Conor asked.

"It'll only take us about three hours to drive to the penitentiary. We can do it in a day. Who's in?" Kyle asked, clearly up for the road trip.

"Me," Julia called.

Conor wasn't so sure. "Shouldn't we wait until after the custody hearing, in case we're needed here?"

"We'll leave early to be there when visiting hours begin and be home mid-afternoon," Kyle assured him.

"I guess that's not so bad. But the guy might not even speak to us."

"Let me handle that," Julia said, making Conor wonder what she intended to do. "He won't say no to a young woman who's found a box of evidence squirreled away by the beloved Great-Aunt Sophia."

Conor nodded. "That might do it."

"I'll go call," Julia said with a wink and stood then went into the kitchen.

"Sometimes I wonder about her." Kyle laughed.

"Me too."

CHAPTER NINE

Conor

The drive to the prison hadn't been too bad. They'd left early as planned and were now in the visitor waiting area hoping Father Henry Jones appeared through the doors directly in front of them.

Conor had been to a prison before as part of his job, but Julia and Kyle looked slightly overwhelmed. It might've been all the bars and security doors they'd walked through, or the thorough search when they arrived, but he was betting the looks some inmates had given them while they'd walked to visitors' room had ratcheted up their nerves. Prison wasn't a local jail where old Joe could sleep off his bender. This place housed some of the most dangerous offenders in order to keep society safe.

Also, there was the sign on the wall that read: "All contraband you've stashed in any of your body's orifices will be found one way or another." It always amazed him to see what people tried to smuggle into these places. He remembered hearing about a guy in North Carolina who stowed a .38 caliber handgun in his rectum, and it was found in his cell the next day. The thought of it made Conor cringe.

He could hear people headed their way, and moments later, the door opened, revealing a thin elderly man and a correctional officer laughing as they entered.

"Here you go, Henry. These are the people here to visit you," the guard said before taking up a position near the back wall.

Henry was in his late seventies and walked with a slight limp. He had a full head of white hair and a friendly smile.

"Hello, I'm Henry Jones. You know Sophia?"

"Knew," Julia said. "She passed away."

A strange look crossed Henry's face, but he said nothing.

"Would you like to sit down?" Conor asked as he motioned at the empty chair. "We'd like to talk to you about Sophia and what we've found at the lake house."

Henry took a moment before taking a seat. Three people visiting him out of the blue had to be perplexing.

"I'm not sure I'm of any help to you young people. Sophia and I were friends a long time ago. God rest her soul."

"I'm Conor. These are my friends, Julia and Kyle. We live at the lake house along with Sophia's great-nephew, Christopher Matthews."

"It's still in the family's hands?" Henry asked.

"Yes. Brick, Christopher, has been busy restoring and renovating the place," Julia said. "She left it to him."

"That's good. Sophia loved that place."

"We all love that place." Julia smiled, which elicited one from the priest.

"Mr. Jones, when we began removing things from the house, we found boxes of information on you and the shooting death of Jericho Miles," Kyle explained.

Henry nodded and said, "I was pretty big news for a while. Lots of newspapers covered the killer priest."

"It's more than newspaper clippings. A coroner's report and files from the old sheriff's station were saved before being destroyed when they leveled the building and built the new station. There's so much information it's hard to understand why she kept it all," Conor said, hoping Henry would have more insight.

"If you're looking for information from me, I'm sorry, but I don't have any answers for you. I've been in here a long time."

"Why did you shoot Jericho?" Kyle jumped in.

"I had my reasons."

"How well did you know Sophia?" Julia asked.

"I'd been sent to the town straight out of the seminary. Sophia was one of the first people to welcome me and helped me get the lay of the land. We'd known each other for over a year before the incident."

"Sounds like Sophia," Julia said.

"She was a kind young woman back then," Henry continued.

"By all accounts, that never stopped," Conor said.

"I didn't think it would. Sophia possessed a great deal of empathy for her fellow man."

"No one saw you shoot Jericho. You could have remained silent," Conor stated. "Why did you confess?"

"Remaining silent was not an option. My faith required me to come forward."

"It had to be one hell of a reason to have someone with your values take a life," Julia said. "I'm sorry it came to that."

Henry nodded once again but stayed quiet, looking as if he was deep in thought.

Kyle tried another way to get the priest to talk. "There's no reason not to tell us. Most, if not all, of the people in Marshall back then have either moved or died. Secrets or promises must've reached some kind of statute of limitations by now."

"Why does this interest you three this much? It was done and over a long time ago."

"Because Sophia wants us to figure it out," Julia answered. "She left all of this for someone to find for a reason, and we're going to figure it out."

Henry smiled and stood. "Sophia would have liked you three, but as for helping you, I've got nothing to add. I'm sorry you came all this way."

The guard came over and led Henry from the room. Conor wasn't sure how to feel. They'd met the man at the center of the mystery and had nothing to show for it. No new information or leads. Nothing.

"Well, this sucks," Kyle stated.

"It sure does," Julia agreed before standing. "What a waste."

Conor noticed a man wearing a suit looking in their direction as he entered the room. "This may not be over yet."

"What?" Kyle asked, and Conor stood and took up position in front of the other two.

He didn't know what was happening, but he'd be the first to face it. This wasn't Julia's or Kyle's world. Conor had been the one who'd spent a great deal of time in some of the sketchiest, not-so-legal places.

"Hello," the guy said as he stopped before them. "I'm Assistant Warden Renaldo Gomez, and I'd like to have a word with you three in my office."

"Mr. Gomez, what's this about?" Conor asked.

"I have a few questions that perhaps you can answer. Please, follow me."

Conor nodded his agreement, and the three followed the assistant warden out of the visitation room and down a long hallway. This wasn't what he'd expected to happen today, but he'd roll with it.

Mr. Gomez turned into what had to be his office at the end of the hallway. Conor had noticed that he kept his pace slow in deference to Kyle using his walker to ambulate.

"Please have a seat," he instructed while rounding his desk.

They did as asked and waited while the warden opened a thick file on his desk.

"How do you know the preacher?" Gomez asked.

"The preacher?" Conor asked right back.

"Yes, Henry Jones."

"I thought he'd been excommunicated from the church?" Julia asked.

"He was, but that doesn't stop him from preaching the good word to anyone willing to listen. Model prisoner since day one. Mostly."

"We don't know him personally, only by the information we found regarding him shooting another man," Kyle explained.

Something was bugging Conor. "Why hasn't the 'preacher' been granted parole after all these years?" He found it interesting that Henry wouldn't've been released by now. Hell, fifty-four years was a long time, even with a life sentence, which typically sees parole eligibility after twenty-five years.

"The answer to that is a story within itself, but first, please tell me why you are interested in Henry Jones."

"We live in a lake house that used to belong to a friend's great-aunt, Sophia Matthews. We found old newspaper clippings regarding the case," Julia explained, apparently not wanting to give away too much. "Sophia and Henry appear to have been friends before the shooting."

Renaldo flipped through the file, and when he found the page he'd been searching for, he smiled before turning it around so they could all see it. There on the page was a log of visitors for Henry Jones, and every Tuesday, there was one name who signed in, Sophia Matthews.

"How long had she been visiting him?" Conor asked.

"The log goes back fifty years."

"Sophia drove all this way to meet with Henry?" Julia questioned.

"Yes. It appears she never missed a Tuesday until roughly five years ago."

"Sophia died two years before into this timeline," Conor said as he looked up from the log. "Her nephew inherited and moved in shortly after she passed away. It's been almost three years since he took possession of the house. Timing sounds about right," Conor confirmed.

"Henry neglected to mention she'd visited," Kyle said.

"No surprise. He refuses to discuss anything about her or the shooting. And to answer your question about parole, for every year he's been eligible, he's refused to apply for a parole hearing. The one time the prison scheduled it on his behalf, Henry stabbed another inmate," the assistant warden explained.

"He stabbed someone?" Julia's brows nearly went up to her hairline.

"It was nothing more than a surface wound. It didn't even require stitches. However, it was good enough to stop his parole hearing and add another charge to his file in addition to years on his sentence to be eligible for parole. Strangest thing, he stabbed one of his best friends."

"What did the guy who got stabbed say about it?" Conor asked.

"Not much. He said Henry cut him with a sharpened toothbrush we found in Henry's cell. Henry admitted to doing it and provided no reason why."

"Weird," Kyle said.

"If you think that's weird, they're still friends to this day."

"It was a setup," Conor said. "He didn't want to be paroled."

"The question is why?" Renaldo asked.

"Could be he's been in so long he can't handle life on the outside," Conor stated.

"That's sad," Julia said.

"Or he thinks he doesn't deserve the freedom after what he did," Kyle added.

"One way or the other, at this point, Henry Jones will die in prison," Renaldo stated.

"Do you think Sophia and Henry were more than friends?" Julia asked.

"It's possible," Conor said.

"Sophia never married," Julia muttered. "And her nephew was her closest relative."

Kyle shook his head. "Still, from what we know, things don't add up."

"That's why I hoped you'd have some answers," Renaldo said.

"We may not have all the answers yet, but this is far from over," Conor assured the warden.

"Why do you care so much?" Kyle asked.

Renaldo took a deep breath and seemed to be deciding how much to say. "Henry Jones saved my life during a riot ten years back."

"How?" Conor asked.

"Henry was collecting the bibles from his Sunday mass, and I was in the next room when the alarms went off. I knew there was no way to reach the guard station in time when Henry came charging into the room. I thought the worst, but he told me to hide under the desk since it had front and side panels, and no one would see me unless they came around to the other side. Then Henry sat behind the desk, opened his bible, and began reading as if nothing was wrong."

"What happened?" Kyle asked.

"Every time a prisoner came running into the room, Henry reported that he was the only one there reading his bible and offered to read the good word with them. The riot went on for hours before we regained control, and I was no longer in danger."

"You owe him your life," Conor stated.

"I believe I do."

As they were leaving the prison Julia said, "We came here for answers, but all we got was more questions."

CHAPTER TEN

Gunner

Gunner watched the star-filled sky as it lightened with the approaching sunrise. Soon, with the first bits of yellow, red, and orange, the world would wake up to a new day. As for Gunner, he'd barely said good-bye to yesterday, and his lack of sleep was riding him hard.

It'd been weeks since he'd slept more than four hours in a row, and if he were a regular Joe, it would've been enough to do some damage. But he'd been trained to within an inch of his life, and he knew how to continue functioning while suffering from extreme exhaustion. At least there was no threat of him losing his shit due to some psychosis brought on by lack of sleep. Four hours a night was a luxury when he was on a mission.

Gunner had spent years in some of the world's most hostile, uninhabitable places, and still managed to sleep. Now his nightmares came too close to reality, especially when it came to his fear of losing Ben. Weird dreams infiltrated his brain: one minute he was back on the battlefield lining up the crosshairs of his sniper's rifle, and when the mark turned around, it was Ben looking back at him.

It happened almost every time he closed his eyes. One time Ben's the target, the next, he's a child victim the team found in a bombed-out village destroyed by the enemy. Or Ben became the enemy firing his M16 at Gunner. His sleep felt like his personal nine circles of hell.

Birds began chirping in the trees as he leaned back in his chair on the porch and closed his eyes. The happy little fuckers were getting on his nerves. Why could he always fall asleep when he knew he'd have to be up at any moment? It was torture.

"Why don't you go back to bed?" Conor asked from somewhere behind him.

Gunner wasn't caught off guard. He never was caught off guard. He'd heard Conor's footsteps long before the guy walked out onto the porch.

Conor had a distinctive gait, which was true about most people, and Gunner could distinguish one from another. Conor's gait was only one of the things Gunner found distinctive and unique about the man.

"I have to get up soon anyway. There's no use bothering," Gunner grumbled.

"I'll take care of Ben while you get a few hours of sleep," Conor offered. "I promise not to leave his side."

"Thanks, but it won't make a difference. I can't sleep."

"Have you tried my grandma's tea?"

"No." Why would he drink tea? He needed a heavy tranquilizer, not weeds in hot water.

"She swears by it. I can make you a pot."

"Tea isn't going to work." Unless there was a truckload they could dump on his head.

"How can you be so sure?"

"Man, give it up. Nothing short of being hit over the head into unconsciousness will work."

"Wanna bet?"

That got his attention. "There's nothing illegal in this tea, is there?" That was all he needed, to get caught high as a teenage stoner.

"Of course not. My grams is a whiz with herbs and things. I asked her to make up a blend a couple of days ago in case you needed it. If you try, I promise to watch over Ben."

"If I try the damn tea will you shut up about it?"

"Yeah."

"Okay, but if I try the magic potion, I believe you mentioned something about a bet. I want something when it doesn't work."

"What?"

"I'll let you know, but it'll involve grocery shopping."

"Believe me, the tea works."

"Don't keep yammering. I said I'll play along."

"Fine, I accept your challenge," Conor stated sharply. "I'll tell you what I want after you wake up."

"Let's do this."

Gunner followed Conor into the house to find the kettle already boiling.

"Pretty sure of yourself."

"I knew the moment you heard the word 'bet' you'd be all over it." Conor laughed as he made a beeline for the kettle.

Gunner chuckled but didn't reply. If he was getting predictable, that was a bad sign. It meant Conor knew him too well already.

Watching Conor mix the brew, and then strain out the twigs and flowers, didn't help boost the concoction's efficacy. When he handed over the mug, Gunner had second thoughts Conor must've read.

"A deal's a deal. Suck it back and get some rest."

Gunner let out a deep huff, squared his stance, suspecting the tea to taste god-awful, and tipped the mug back in one shot.

"Be careful. It's hot."

Gunner didn't care. He wanted to get this over with so he could claim his prize: dinner with Conor. He knew what Conor had said, and it made sense, but something new and unwelcome was running Gunner: his heart wasn't listening to his head.

"There, done," Gunner said before handing over the mug.

"It's not going to knock you out standing there. You have to go lie down and try to rest in bed."

Gunner rolled his eyes and turned to the stairs. "This isn't going to work."

"Go," Conor ordered with a bit of force while pointing to the staircase. "Lie down for ten minutes. I'll time you. If you're not asleep when I check on you, you win."

He could do that. "Fine. The sooner this is over, the sooner you'll shut up about it."

Gunner wanted to storm up the stairs, but everyone was still sleeping, so he vetoed the idea and glared at Conor as he followed him to his bedroom. Once there, he sat on his bed to remove his boots while Conor closed the drapes and removed the clock on his side table.

He played along. Removing his shirt came next, and then his jeans without giving Conor a chance to look away.

"See something you like?"

"Shut up and get in the damn bed."

"Now who's grouchy?"

Conor stormed over, lifted the covers, and said, "Get in."

Gunner raised his hands in mock surrender and did as he was told. Conor dumped the covers over him and turned to leave.

"Answer me this," Gunner said. "Why do you care so much?"

Conor stopped, but didn't turn to look at Gunner, and he thought the man wouldn't respond.

"Because I do."

"That's not an answer."

"It's as good as you're going to get."

Conor shut the door as he left, leaving Gunner to his thoughts. He'd wait the ten minutes, and when he won, he'd continue this conversation over dinner. He imagined how angry Conor would be at losing and smiled wide when he thought of the expression on Conor's face when Gunner walked out of his bedroom wide awake.

As he thought about his prize, his eyes began closing and his body relaxed into the mattress. Then sleep took him in its fickle grip, and happily, he drifted away, dreaming of what he'd cook for their dinner.

***

Conor

He'd never heard the lake house so quiet. After everyone had gotten up, they went into the kitchen, grabbed breakfast, and vacated the property, knowing Gunner had finally fallen asleep. Construction on the cottages was at a standstill until their teammate woke. They knew how bent out of shape he was about the hearing, and how badly he needed to catch up on his sleep.

Conor had made an extra-strong batch of tea to knock out the big guy. Given his size and profession, he wasn't the garden-variety patient, and a little extra insurance never hurt.

"You going to explain why you made a deal with the Don?" Grandma asked.

The two were sitting on the porch watching the kids play while some of the team went fishing and others relaxed around the property on one of their only days off in a long while. They needed it.

This was the first time the two of them were alone, and grams wasn't holding back.

"Because nothing I was doing worked, and I had to try everything possible to keep Ben safe and with Gunner."

"You'll owe that psycho a favor."

"I'm well aware of the parameters of the agreement."

"Don't get all haughty with me, young man."

"Sorry, ma'am."

"I'm worried."

"So am I."

"But I doubt it's for the same reason. I'm worried Don Reza will request something horrible for the information you seek."

"I'm worried Ben will be taken away, destroying his life and his uncle's."

"You're risking your future to save these people. While the cause is surely worth it, the Don isn't exactly a trustworthy person to deal with."

"A favor for a favor. That's the deal I agreed to and will stand by. You know I have to do this. I can't allow something horrible to happen to Ben. I would never be able to live with myself if I didn't do all I could."

She looked at him and sighed. "Why do you always have to do the right thing?"

Conor smiled, knowing his grams understood. "Because you raised me that way."

"Don't blame me for this." She scowled, but he knew she didn't mean it. "This is about that gift of yours. We'll figure this out when Ben is safe with his uncle."

"Thanks for understanding." Conor wrapped his arm around his grandma's shoulders.

"Just because I understand doesn't mean I'm not still angry with you." She slapped his leg without any heat. She understood more than most why Conor was compelled to deal with the Don.

"You love me. You could never stay mad at me for long."

"You're right, I love you, but you're pushing it with this stunt."

"What stunt?" Brick asked as he turned the corner onto the porch. His tone brooked no arguments.

Shit.

Grandma stood and looked at Brick with a stone-cold stare Conor had only seen a handful of times. "You shut down all those nasty thoughts in your head right now. My grandson is a brave, strong, and caring man who risked himself and got sucked into a big honkin' mess. He doesn't need your constant suspicions."

Brick stopped in his tracks. "I'm sorry, ma'am, but I'm trained to be suspicious."

"Grandma, it's okay." She gave him "the look." "Please go in and make a pot of coffee. Gunner should be waking up soon." She tilted her head but looked unmoved. "Please."

She shot Brick another "don't-fuck-with-me" glare and walked back into the house. One crisis averted, and on to the next. It seemed like Conor was always putting out fires, and it was getting old.

CHAPTER ELEVEN

Conor

Conor brought Brick up to date. The team leader sat listening without uttering a word, and in the end, sat silently as Conor asked, "You can't tell Gunner. Please. I can't promise to deliver something that maybe could help, but I can't seem to find. He's going through enough."

Brick turned his dark piercing eyes on Conor. "Why are you doing this?"

"I've already explained."

"Yeah, I get the whole adopted thing, but this is above and beyond."

"It's something I need to do for them."

"Is this about Gunner or Ben?"

"Both. They are inseparable in my mind."

Brick looked off into the distance before saying, "You've thought this through?"

"Yeah. I accept my fate if the Don finds him."

"We'll see," Brick growled before standing and walking off the porch and headed toward the cottages.

"What is it with that phrase and this team?"

Brick didn't answer. Conor hadn't expected him to.

They were a peculiar bunch.

***

Gunner

Gunner hadn't felt this good in months. It was amazing what uninterrupted sleep could do for a person. The nightmares had remained at bay, and he considered getting the tea recipe because he could foresee a lot of sleepless nights in his future.

Though he appreciated the rest, he'd lost the bet, which meant he wouldn't be having a private dinner with Conor. He'd hoped to show off his cooking prowess and introduce Conor to one of Gunner's home country's favorite dishes.

It'd been two days since their bet, and Conor still hadn't told him what he wanted. The pain in his ass was keeping him waiting. Gunner had patience a plenty, but was curious to find out what Conor wanted most of all.

As time got closer to the court date, Gunner and Ben spent all their time together. He tried shaking the feeling of impending doom, but it was always lurking in the background. At times it was all-consuming, and he had to pull himself out of his head before Ben noticed. It was tiring being this stressed out while pretending everything was all right.

"Let's go."

Gunner looked up from the board he was measuring to find Conor standing there.

"Go where?"

"I've decided what I want for my win."

Gunner stood. "And what exactly is that?"

"I've decided I want you to cook a Czech meal for everyone."

"What?" The ask was eerily close to what Gunner had originally wanted, minus the rest of the team and their visitors. But he'd take what he could get.

"I've been told you are quite the chef, and I want to see and taste what you can do."

Gunner was starting to understand Conor and the way he did things. It appeared he was patient and had a sharp memory. He remembered mentioning wanting a home-cooked meal from his homeland a long time ago at breakfast, and Conor was going to make it happen, even if Gunner had to cook it.

"Okay, I'll get cleaned up, grab Ben, and we'll be off."

Conor smiled, making Gunner do the same. Other team members were working nearby and had overheard the conversation.

"What are you cooking for us?" Fletch asked.

Gunner shrugged his shoulders and looked at Conor. "What do you want me to cook?"

"Something homey and hearty."

"Beef goulash and dumplings it is."

"Yesss," Shaw hissed in happiness. "We haven't had that in forever."

Gunner felt lighter with every passing moment, and soon the three of them were off to town to do some grocery shopping. Ben sat in his car seat in the back of the quad cab and Conor sat in the passenger seat. More than once, Gunner caught himself imagining things better left alone because it could all be gone soon enough.

"Oh, there's a second part to my winning," Conor said.

"And that is?"

"For the next few hours, I want you to live in this moment only. No thinking beyond what we are doing right now."

"That might be hard to do."

"All I'm asking is for you to try. Take one night off from worry and stress. It'll be there tomorrow."

Gunner thought about it and wondered if he could block out all the shit coming his way and enjoy the night.

With a reassuring look at Ben in his rearview mirror, he had his answer. "Sure. I can try."

"That's all I ask."

Gunner reached across the center console and took hold of Conor's hand.

"I meant what I said. Now's not the time for you to make decisions," Conor stated but didn't pull away.

"I'm not down on bended knee. We're holding hands. I'm sure that doesn't break any of your rules."

***

Conor

Conor looked down at their joined hands and couldn't bring himself to pull away. Gunner's hand was warm and calloused from hard work, and nothing had ever felt so good.

"No, I guess not."

"Good," Gunner responded and squeezed Conor's hand.

He felt like a damned teenager holding hands with his high school crush. He was a grown man who'd had lovers, and yet this felt different from anything he'd ever experienced. Deeper. More meaningful. Before he could examine it too closely, they arrived on the outskirts of the small town of Marshall.

Pretty as a postcard in many ways, it had well-tended houses with sweeping yards, a football stadium, quaint schools, and small mom-and-pop shops. There was Gator's Bar, a fair-sized grocery store, a library, a couple of banks, a pharmacy, and other essentials needed to lead a happy small-town life.

He watched it all pass with a yearning he'd never known. Strange how circumstances changed one's point of view. He was a die-hard East Coast urbanite lusting after a life in a small Texas town he could never have.

They pulled into the grocery store parking lot, which was half filled with cars and trucks.

"We're here," Ben announced. "Can we get ice cream for Matthew and me?"

"Yeah, buddy," Gunner said. "You guys earned a treat from doing all your chores around the house."

Conor turned to look at Ben and the young boy beamed under his uncle's praise. Their connection was solid, which would allow Ben to live a happy and carefree life. If Conor did nothing else before leaving here, he'd make certain Ben got that life.

They walked into the grocery store and grabbed a shopping cart. It was going to take a lot of food to feed the crew at the lake house. Each of those guys ate enough for two people. Conor lifted Ben into the front of the cart and began pushing it behind a determined-looking Gunner. Apparently, the man took shopping seriously.

"So where do we begin, lord of the feast?" Conor asked while waving his arm like some game show model toward the aisles of food.

Gunner smiled. He'd been doing a lot more of that recently, and Conor wanted it to continue.

"Good meat is where it all begins for *cesky gulas*."

"To the meat cooler." Conor stuck out his arm as if he had a sword pointing in the direction of the next aisle, making Ben laugh loudly.

They hadn't been far from the meat section, and in a matter of moments, Gunner was eyeing up some choice cuts of beef. He took his time deciding which would make it into their feast. Conor enjoyed watching Gunner concentrate on his task. The man was focused.

Once he'd decided on the protein, they were off to the spice aisle. Paprika, garlic, and dried marjoram were added to the cart. He had no idea what marjoram was, but Gunner seemed stoked the store stocked it. Then they were off to grab a bag of onions and a few cans of tomato paste.

"I almost forgot about the *knedliky*," Gunner said as he scanned the aisles.

Conor pulled out his phone, opened the new app he'd downloaded, and said, "*Knedliky*."

The computerized voice said, "Czech dumplings."

Gunner gave him a sidelong glance.

"What?" Conor asked.

"You downloaded a Czech-to-English translator?"

"How else would I be able to understand half of what you're saying?"

"No one has ever bothered."

"Well, I'm thorough. We've already established that."

"I like thorough," Gunner said before turning. "To the flour aisle."

"And the ice cream, right?" Ben asked, sounding hopeful.

"Of course, buddy," Gunner replied. "But we'll get it last so it doesn't melt on us."

Ben's smile was back in place.

"Your Uncle Gunner always keeps his word, kiddo."

"Promise?"

"Promise."

They were off in search of a coarse flour that would mix quick or something along those lines. Conor wasn't a chef, and the nuances of putting a complicated meal together were lost on him.

"Ah, here, this will do nicely," Gunner said as he placed a large bag in the cart.

"How many dumplings are you planning on making?" Conor eyed the bag.

"Whatever is left can be used up in other ways. Besides, you'll love it and insist I cook it on the regular," Gunner stated.

"Good point." Conor didn't have the heart to say otherwise.

If Ben's father was found, Conor would owe Don Reza a favor and likely have to leave. If the judge ruled in Gunner's favor, Conor wouldn't have to leave, but it seemed the most likely outcome. And, though he hated to think of it, if the opposite result came to pass, Gunner wouldn't be in any shape to cook for anyone.

Conor grabbed a carton of blueberries from the produce display, and handed it to Ben. "Eat up, kid. Dinner might take a while from the looks of this cart."

"Thanks," Ben said as he cracked the top.

"It's barely two in the afternoon. Dinner is hours away. Maybe we should stop for something to eat," Gunner suggested.

"Ben already had lunch, so a snack or two will get him through to dinner. Besides, I have a feeling there's going to be an abundance of food tonight." He patted his stomach. "I'm saving room to gorge."

Gunner grinned. "Okay, but let's grab a bunch of bananas. Ben loves them to snack on."

"Already done," Conor said as he pointed to the cart. "Picked them up when we went through produce."

Again with the sidelong glance. Gunner's expression was unreadable, but now wasn't the time to ask what the glance meant. Conor would have to remember to ask after Ben went to bed.

"Yeast."

"Yeast?"

"We need it for the dumplings," Gunner said.

"To the yeast," Ben said around a mouth filled with blueberries.

"You got it, buddy." Gunner ruffled the kid's hair.

An older lady with gray hair tied up in a tidy bun who had a cane hanging from her cart turned down their aisle, and Conor moved their cart over to the side so she could pass. Instead, she stopped beside them.

"Hello there, sweetie," she said as she held out a wrapped red lollipop to Ben.

Ben looked to Gunner for direction. "You can take it, Ben. Remember to say thank you."

With an even bigger smile, Ben took the offered candy and did as he was told.

"You're welcome, young man." She smiled, and then turned her attention to Conor and Gunner. "A mighty fine family you got here. Don't ever let them tell you otherwise."

She patted Gunner's arm, smiled at Conor, and went on her way.

Conor looked at Gunner to gauge his reaction, but he'd already turned away and headed farther down the aisle.

So much for making the shopping trip light and fun.

Conor hoped the family comment hadn't ruined the rest of the day.

CHAPTER TWELVE

Gunner

As they drove home, Gunner was dealing with an odd realization. The lady in the grocery store saw it before he had. They behaved like a family. Everything had been comfortable and easy between them as they shopped the aisles, and he'd fallen into the kind of contentment he'd never had. He knew he wanted Conor, but he hadn't gotten past the sex. The old lady put a line under the obvious.

Odd to think this way when his entire life was in a holding pattern where the bottom could fall out. He refused to focus on the potential crash and burn. He had to keep a good thought. He couldn't and wouldn't see past a happy result.

"Hey, where are all the vehicles?" Conor asked as they pulled into the driveway. "The place looks deserted."

Gunner scanned the area but didn't pick up any movement. "Huh. Where'd they go?"

His phone pinged, and he picked it up out of the cup holder.

Brick: *Have a good night.*

"We've been ghosted."

"What?"

"Everyone's cleared out," Gunner said and showed Conor the text.

"Why would they do that?"

"Because my team knows what I need most."

Conor quirked up a brow and looked confused.

"It'll be a peaceful evening with only the three of us."

"What about all this food?"

"It'll keep. I'll cook more than we'll eat and freeze the rest. Trust me. It won't last long."

"Hmm, okay."

Gunner parked the truck, and the three of them unloaded the groceries. Ben insisted he help, so they gave him the extra special job of carrying important things like bread, ice cream, blueberries, and bananas.

Once they got everything inside the unusually quiet house, Gunner began preparing the dough and cutting the meat into inch-wide cubes. Conor and Ben had set up one of his nephew's favorite board games, Pictureka, on the coffee table. The object was to find certain pictures in a square full of crazy characters. Ben loved it.

Before long, Gunner could hear them laughing as he removed the browned meat and then softened the onions in the same pot. The dough for the dumplings was rising, and the goulash was well on its way. So he took a few minutes to join the game.

"Who's winning?" he asked as he sat on the couch beside Ben.

"Who do you think?" Conor teased.

"Ben, of course."

"Yay," Ben cheered. "I can find the pictures fast."

"I have no doubt. You have eagle eyes like me," Gunner said.

"How's dinner coming?"

"It's well on its way. Everything will be ready by six."

"Do we know where everyone disappeared to for the night?"

"I'm guessing down the road to Roman's father's place, or over to Shaw, Bryan, and Kyle's ranch."

"Don't the women from the sauce business live there?" He remembered something about Kyle going into business with the women who'd been saved from the human trafficking ring.

"Yeah. The place is huge, and there's still plenty of room for them to expand. The women are comfortable with the team and have cooked for us often."

"Lucky you. You want to jump into our game?"

"Play with us, Uncle Gunner," Ben said.

Gunner looked back into the kitchen. There wasn't anything he had to do for about fifteen minutes. "Sure, for a little while."

"Okay. Pick a card," Ben instructed.

Gunner reached for the colored dice and rolled a green. He couldn't help but notice the happiness on Conor's and Ben's faces, and thought he should have this all the time.

"How many do you need to find?" Ben asked.

This time Gunner picked up the dice and rolled a four. "Okay, I need to find four what?" He took the top card on the deck and flipped it over, exposing the word teeth. He spun the timer over, and the sand began to trickle down to the bottom. "Four teeth in thirty seconds. Got it."

Gunner stood over the coffee table, scanning and pointing as he found the correct pictures. "There. One there. Here's another, and this one here makes four."

"You got it." Ben jumped into his arms. "I knew you would."

Click.

Gunner turned to find Conor taking a picture of them. "Whatcha doing?"

"I thought it'd be nice to have a few pictures to hang on the walls of your new cottage."

There was something innately kind about Conor. Not a pushover by any stretch of the imagination, but honest and real in his desire to make people feel good about themselves. He cared for people on a different level than most and strove to do meaningful things. The complete opposite of what Gunner had thought when they first met.

"Thanks." Their gazes locked, and he couldn't force himself to look away. He noticed the green flecks in Conor's eyes.

"You're welcome."

"Uncle Gunner, I think something's burning," Ben shouted, breaking their connection.

He stood and ran to the stove to find a piece of paper towel he'd left too close to the burner was beginning to singe. Gunner threw it into the sink and turned on the water. He knew better than to leave a stovetop for any length of time. He'd been so involved with playing with Ben, he'd been careless.

"Everything okay?"

Gunner turned to find Conor standing a few feet away. "Yeah. A paper towel was too close to the stove. Food's all good."

"Phew. I'm starving." Conor smile deescalated Gunner's self-recrimination.

"Good, I made enough for seconds."

"I'm sure the others will dig into all the leftovers. They made it clear: they love your cooking."

"I cooked for the team when we were back on base with whatever I could find since rations only go so far when you're craving home-cooked food."

"That's amazing."

Gunner rubbed the back of his neck and said, "I guess."

"No guessing about it. You gave them the best meal you could put together while deployed who knows where. I'm sure they appreciated your efforts."

He'd never looked at it that way. It was just something he did. Gunner closed the distance between them. He couldn't help it. The pull was too strong not to.

"I know what you said before about this not being the right time, and I agree, but for tonight, could you put that aside and be here with me?"

"For a man of few words, you certainly have a way with them," Conor said, considering he'd asked Gunner to let everything go for one night. "For tonight, sure. But tomorrow we go back to the status quo."

"That's all I ask," Gunner said before closing the distance and leaning in to kiss Conor. Those soft lips could easily become an addiction.

"Uncle Gunner, why are you kissing Uncle Conor?" Ben asked with the innocence of a child.

"Because we care about each other, buddy."

"Like Uncle Brick and Uncle Roman?"

Gunner looked to Conor to answer this one. He already knew where he stood, and that was all in. Gunner'd had time to think about all the factors involved, and his position didn't change.

They belonged together.

He felt it with his whole being.

***

Conor

With Ben and Gunner looking at him, Conor went with the truth. "Yep. Just like them."

"Okay. Can I have a juice box?"

Leave it to Ben to make things simple. If only.

"Yeah, buddy. The apple juice boxes are in the fridge on the bottom rack."

"'Kay."

How wonderful the outside pressures of people who didn't see love and caring as the pure best things they were hadn't filtered in to affect the little guy's understanding of what he knew and felt from the family around him. If you cared about each other, that was all that mattered. No questions or comments were necessary, only simple acceptance.

The world could learn a lot from children.

"Come on, Uncle Conor, we're still playing the game."

"Be right there."

Before he turned to leave, Conor leaned in and kissed Gunner without a second thought. When he looked back, Gunner still stood there with a goofy smile.

For tonight he'd let it go. All of it. The fear of losing Ben, the favor from the Don, which meant a favor for the Don, finding Ben's father, and dealing with the in-laws from hell. The fact they hadn't even requested a visit with Ben was telling. He hoped the judge saw this shit for what it was.

"You like my uncle?" Ben asked when Conor sat on the couch.

"Yep. He's a wonderful person, and he loves you very much."

"Will you be moving into the cottage with us?"

"That's not in the works, kid."

"Uncle Gunner is happy now. It's okay if you did." Even the kid wasn't immune to fixing them up.

Conor reached over and tousled the boy's dark hair. "Don't ever change. You're perfect the way you are."

That had Ben smiling.

Conor looked over at Gunner working away in the kitchen. He could do this and live out a dream for one night.

Maybe the angels would be on their side and everything would all work out somehow.

Or perhaps he could come back after he was forced to repay the Don's favor.

Though the odds were slim on either count.

So, for one night Conor would hold tight to hope.

CHAPTER THIRTEEN

Conor

Conor looked down at the deep bowl filled to the brim with thick cubes of beef and dark gravy, and breathed in the aromas of Gunner's homeland. The hefty dumplings had been cut, ready to soak up all that goodness, and Conor could barely hold back as they waited for Gunner to join them.

"All right, dig in," Gunner said, and Conor didn't need to be told twice.

Ben was happily dunking his dumpling in the gravy while Conor groaned. The tender beef melted in his mouth, and the thick, luscious, perfectly spiced gravy was drinkable. The caramelized onions added a tang of flavor, but the true *pièce de résistance* was when he dipped a wedge of dumpling in the creamy gravy, added the meat and onions, and ate it all at once.

"Beef goulash is amazing," Conor said to the chef. "You were right. We'll need lots more of this, or as much as Rick allows us." They both laughed, knowing that wouldn't fly too often.

"*Perfektni*. That's what I wanted to hear," Gunner said with his chest puffed out.

"It's yummy," Ben agreed as he shoveled more gravy-soaked dumpling into his mouth.

"Eat up. There's plenty. And if we have room, we'll have some ice cream before bedtime."

"Yesss," Ben hissed in happiness. Something he'd picked up from one of the team for sure.

They tucked into their meals and didn't come up for conversation until their goulash was gobbled up.

"Do you want some more?" Gunner asked as Conor wiped his plate clean with a piece of dumpling.

"You bet. I'll get it. Sit and relax."

Gunner nodded.

Conor set his plate on the counter and went to get the pot when he noticed the lack of dirty dishes in the sink.

"Hey. You already rinsed the dishes and put them in the dishwasher?"

"You bet."

"Haven't you ever heard of the cook not having to do the dishes?"

"I find it easier to clean as I go."

"Well, don't touch any other dishes 'cause I'm going to do them."

"Okay, okay," Gunner said, raising his arms in surrender, but he couldn't hide his grin.

Hell, we do sound like an old married couple.

***

Gunner

We do sound like an old married couple.

No wonder the lady at the store thought they were a family. Gunner appreciated what she'd said, and felt more hopeful than he had a right to feel. Sure, most of the community was cool, but there were some dye-in-the-wool bigots about town. But more, he knew he stood on shifting sand until the hearing was over. Until then, he couldn't contemplate the concept of his own family.

He watched as Conor brought more dumplings to the table and bent to cut pieces for Ben. Conor fit in so perfectly. He'd promised the man he'd let all the shit go for tonight, and that's what he'd do. One night of pretend domesticated bliss.

"What's wrong?"

"Nothing. Lost in thought."

"No thinking. Remember?"

"Right. A momentary lapse."

"Good. Don't let it happen again."

"Yes, sir."

Conor smiled, and Gunner couldn't look away. He'd caused the joy on Conor's face. Most of his adult life, he'd caused men to fear, despise, and run from him, but nothing even close to receiving joy. Knowing he might not be as big a monster as he thought was odd.

Hours later, and each of their bowls of ice cream demolished, Ben was tucked safely in bed, and Gunner and Conor were watching some eighties horror movie that had them both laughing.

"That's it, walk into the dark forest in the middle of the stormy night," Gunner said.

"Why would she want to stay in the safe, warm house when she could be running for her life amongst nature?" Conor deadpanned.

"And here comes the dude with the butcher's knife."

"Seriously. Who carries around a butcher's knife?"

"You never know when you might have to prepare a meal."

"Or a brainless victim."

"True." Gunner laughed.

They were sitting a few feet away from each other on the couch. It was comfortable and easy, but Gunner couldn't fight the urge to get closer to Conor. Reaching over, he grabbed Conor and pulled him to his side.

"You could've asked." Conor chuckled.

"You might've said no."

"Ah, you didn't want to risk it."

"My life has been a study of removing risk."

"And people."

"Yeah."

"That had to be tough."

Gunner was surprised by Conor's reaction. People in his experience were either "what does it feel like to kill someone" or "that's pretty fucked up." Never had anyone considered, not to mention state, that his work had to be hard on him. Only the team knew and understood.

Until now.

Until Conor.

"Tough?"

"Yeah, having to hunt people down on behalf of our government. I don't mean the people were innocent, and there were surely justified reasons certain people were targeted, but still, it must've been difficult carrying the job and them."

"It's my duty." *And my curse.*

"I know, but it's only us here. How are you?"

This was not the way Gunner saw this evening going. "How am I?"

"Yeah. All this new stress must be playing havoc on any existing PTSD you may have suffered from your service."

"What makes you think I have PTSD?" Deflect, deflect, deflect.

"Because you're a good and honorable man, I think taking all those lives, no matter how much it was warranted, would leave its mark."

Gunner couldn't deny that, no matter how much he wanted to. He wasn't psychotic and received no pleasure from his work as a sniper. But it had been his duty, and he shouldered it.

"Sometimes I can still see their faces," Gunner said, and the minute it was out, he regretted it. He didn't want to be a monster, especially to Conor.

"That makes sense," Conor said as he wrapped his arm around Gunner's back.

"It does?"

"Yeah. It'd be hard to watch a person in their last few moments of life, knowing you were there to end it. You're a stronger man than me, that's for sure."

"I wouldn't say that. You never know what you're capable of until you're faced with it."

"You're right. But I still mean what I said. Have you ever talked to anyone about how to deal with those memories?"

"No. I'm good."

"I know you are, but even the strongest person needs someone to talk to about shit like that. You can't keep it buried. It'll make an appearance when you least expect it."

A scream from the TV had them both turning to the movie in time to see some blonde in a towel rearing back from the decapitated body of her boyfriend, who'd been waiting in bed, no doubt. Lesson one, never have sex in a horror movie. You always die.

"Like that," Gunner laughed.

"Something like that."

"Look, I know what you're saying, but I'm not at the point where I can relive all the shit I've been through." He might never be.

"If there comes a time, you know you can talk to me."

"Thanks." He appreciated the offer, but he'd never heave that burden on anyone he cared about. It was bad enough he carried that shit around in his head.

Conor's arm was still around his back, and Gunner thought, *I'm not gonna miss an opportunity to get closer to this desirable man,* so Gunner ran his hand over Conor's stubbled jaw and leaned down for a kiss.

Conor tasted like mint chocolate chip ice cream and coffee. Gunner's new favorite flavor. Their tongues dueled while their hands explored each other's bodies. Excitement coursed through his veins, moving faster with each caress. He wanted Conor with a need he'd never felt, and he wasn't one to stop once he'd found what he wanted.

Slowly, he pushed Conor onto the couch cushions, angling his body until they were both lying flat with Gunner on top of Conor. They never broke the kiss, and continued until both were breathing heavily.

"You know this isn't a smart idea," Conor reminded through gasps for breath.

"I've never been one to take the easy route."

"Well, this won't be remotely easy."

"I'm up for the challenge. You?"

"But you don't know everything."

Gunner thought about it for a moment and decided he didn't care if he had all the information.

"I don't believe you'd do anything to hurt Ben or me."

"Of course not. Never."

"That's all I need to know," Gunner said before he retook Conor's lips and picked up where they left off.

This felt right.

For the first time, Gunner chose what he wanted.

And he wanted Conor.

CHAPTER FOURTEEN

Conor

Conor was dragged under by desire and he didn't fight its pull. He wanted this. He wanted Gunner, and this might be the only chance he'd have. There were no guarantees, and with everything swirling around them, tomorrow wasn't promised to either of them.

At any moment, he or Gunner could be called away. The court hearing was so close, and no one could predict its outcome.

So, for tonight, he intended to take what he desperately wanted before it was too late.

Conor explored Gunner's jean-clad ass before working his way up to his washboard abs and stopping at his broad chest. The man was built, and Conor loved every inch.

Gunner groaned when Conor began undoing the buttons on his shirt and moving his hands to explore the prime real estate of warm flesh over hard muscles. He ran his fingers around nubbed nipples and dipped down to explore an incredibly ripped stomach. He doubted he could ever get enough.

"That feels so good, *milenec*."

"Sorry. Don't have my translator."

"It means lover or boyfriend."

"I like it."

"Thought you might. Do you want to move this up to your room?" Gunner asked. "Ben's is next to mine, so yours would be better."

"My room's good," Conor agreed, causing Gunner to stand and help him up from the couch.

After a quick readjustment to his impossibly hard cock, Conor managed to walk up the stairs and to his bedroom. Gunner had his hand on Conor's waist, assuring him the big guy was right behind him.

The lake house was locked tight for the evening, and there was little chance of them being caught off guard. They locked the door to Conor's room in case Ben wandered in. But they could hear him if he needed anything.

They could barely keep their hands off each other, and now that they were behind closed doors, they tore each other's clothes off with abandon. Caught up in a haze of desire, neither struggled to break free.

Gunner pulled his boxer briefs down his muscled legs and off as Conor admired his long, thick cock pointing directly at him. He wanted all that beauty in his mouth, and went to his knees in front of Gunner. He sucked his lover's cock down his throat while holding on to his fine, toned ass.

"Fuck, yesss," Gunner groaned.

Hearing Gunner's appreciation spurred Conor on as he sucked and licked to his heart's content. Gunner's big hands rested on Conor's head, but not once did he try to force Conor's movements. Knowing the big guy's need for control, the fact that he was holding back meant a lot to the equally dominant Conor.

After lavishing Gunner's cock with special attention, Conor stood, took off his underwear, and wrapped his arms around Gunner's shoulders.

"Last chance to back out," Conor offered.

"No way," Gunner growled before lifting Conor and tossing him onto the bed with a bounce. He wasn't a small man by any barometer, but Gunner was that strong.

Conor lay back against the pillows, put his hands behind his head, and smiled wide. The sight of Gunner standing only a couple of feet away in all his naked, muscled hotness could melt metal. The famous statue of David may have never been if Michelangelo had gotten a look at Gunner. The man was a god.

"Fuck, you're so sexy lying there like that," Gunner said in a deep, scratchy voice.

That comment surprised Conor. "Me? Have you looked in the mirror?"

Gunner crawled into bed, his eyes incredibly dark, and his laser focus was on Conor. It was a heady feeling being the focus of the SEAL's attention, and Conor never wanted to lose it.

"You make me want things I've never dreamed of," Gunner said before changing directions away from Conor's face and moving to his aching cock.

Without stopping, Gunner took Conor's cock into his mouth and growled, sending vibrations rushing through his loins and spreading out to the rest of his body.

"That's it. Oh yeah," Conor mumbled.

Gunner's warm, wet tongue rimmed the engorged head of Conor's cock before dipping into the slit on the end. If he kept that up, Conor was going to come.

"Easy, big guy. Don't want this over before it's begun."

Gunner pulled off and said, "Don't worry, I can get you hard again if you do."

"A challenge. I'm in."

There was a glint in Gunner's eyes before he swallowed Conor down his throat, and sent him flying. Up was down, in was out, and his world was in chaos as every nerve in his body burned with need. His orgasm was bearing down on him fast, and no matter what he did, there was no hope of staving off what came next. Which was him.

He groaned deeply as electricity shot through his bloodstream, and his cock exploded into Gunner's mouth. Conor's head was spinning, and he barely noticed Gunner leap from the bed, pull on his boxers, and leave the room. Seconds later, he returned with supplies that made Conor even happier.

"I'll top this time. You get next," Gunner announced, surprising Conor.

"And here I took you for a diehard top."

"I am, but I'm willing to switch things up with you."

"Really?"

"Don't push it," Gunner huffed. "We'll figure it out together."

"Deal."

Gunner threw the supplies on the bed, ditched the boxer briefs, and rejoined Conor before rolling them both until Conor was lying on top of Gunner. Conor felt a lubed finger circling his hole as their lips locked in another scorching kiss. Gunner's lips swallowed his moan as his desire took flight.

Conor's cast was scheduled to be removed tomorrow, but in this moment, he wished it gone. It kept getting in the way.

"Having problems?" Gunner asked.

"Yeah. I can't move my arm the way I want with this damn thing."

"You get it off tomorrow?"

"Yeah, at eleven."

"It doesn't hurt anymore?"

"No. It's all healed."

"Give it to me," Gunner said, and Conor complied.

He looked at the cast for a moment, and then in a blink of an eye, Gunner tore it in half and tossed it on the floor beside the bed.

"Holy shit. I didn't know that was an option or I would've asked earlier," Conor said as he flexed his stiff wrist and hand. His skin was so pale under where the cast had been.

"It wouldn't've been available to you earlier."

"What? You mean if we weren't about to have sex?"

"No. We're under twelve hours from your appointment to have it sawed off."

"Oh."

"Come here, *milenec*." Gunner chuckled. "You're allowed to question me. It's not as if I haven't given you reason."

"That's in the past. No more second-guessing, right?"

"Right."

Conor dove in for another kiss, and their bodies took over, acting on what they wanted. Conor heard the condom package tear, and he was trying to relax as Gunner slid his two-by-four cock into Conor's body. To say this was the largest dick he'd taken was beyond true, and Gunner seemed to sense it.

He moved slowly and checked in to make sure Conor was okay. Once Gunner's hips touched Conor's ass cheeks, he took a deep breath. His lover dropped his head to take more kisses full of tongue and need, exactly what Conor required as he fully relaxed into their melded bodies.

Gunner's hips flexed before he pulled back a few inches and slid forward. Conor's nerve endings began to fire, and the lube did its job as discomfort morphed into pleasure. Gunner had one arm wrapped around Conor's back and the other holding himself up off Conor.

His head swam with need as he twisted his legs around Gunner's waist and placed his hands against the wooden headboard before pushing into each of Gunner's thrusts. His pleasure skyrocketed as the head of Gunner's cock brushed up against his prostate with every thrust.

To Conor's amazement, he was hard again and about to come... again.

Gunner had been right.

Those incredibly dark eyes felt like they were seeing straight into Conor's soul. He missed nothing, and when his orgasm took over, Gunner drove in deep before Conor's ass clamped down on his lover's cock. A few more thrusts, and Gunner was growling his release into the pillow beside Conor's head.

As they lay entwined, gasping for air, Conor couldn't hold back all he was feeling for Gunner any more than he could hold off a runaway train.

CHAPTER FIFTEEN

Conor

The first two cottages were complete, and Gunner and Ben were preparing to move into the first one with Conor. Julia and Matthew would be moving into the second one right next door, and work would begin on the next two.

The cottages were perfect. Each had two bedrooms, a kitchen, a living room, a playroom, a porch, and two bathrooms. Everything you needed for a happy life, and Conor was happy.

He, Gunner, and Ben had grown even closer.

While things around the lake house were returning to a normal rhythm, Conor, Julia, and Kyle were still actively sorting through the remaining boxes left by Sophia. But it felt like they'd hit a dead end. With Henry Jones unwilling to discuss what happened all those years ago, it looked like whatever Sophia had hoped would happen when the papers were discovered might not. There were a few more names they'd found, and they planned on attempting to find the people involved. They'd agreed, they'd find the truth, and never give up.

Boxes were piling up in all the rooms as Conor began building Ben's new robot bed, Grams was busy organizing their kitchen, and Aunt Viv was doing the same at Julia's. The entire team was helping out, and a party atmosphere was humming below all the activity.

Conor couldn't've been happier.

Until on a busy Tuesday morning, two black, heavily tinted SUVs pulled into the driveway.

"Who's that?" Grams asked.

An icy chill worked through Conor's body when the doors opened.

"Don Reza. I have a feeling he's come to discuss his favor. He must've found Jason."

It'd been nearly two months since he'd reached out, and Conor had been waiting for this day.

Gunner came out of the lake house with Brick by his side. Both went to greet the new arrivals. There appeared to be four bodyguards with Reza. So much for keeping his deal a secret.

"I'll be back in a moment. Please keep Ben here in the cottage."

"I will," his grandmother said. "Please be careful. I love you."

Conor bent to kiss her cheek before turning and heading straight for the Don. This was his responsibility, and he would follow through with their deal. Ben would be safe. Conor would get what he wanted, so the deal would stand.

As he neared the group, he could hear Brick negotiating something with Reza. By the time he reached them, it was all over.

"I accept your offer," Reza said and held out his hand. "We have a deal."

When Brick shook his hand, Conor got a sick feeling in the pit of his stomach.

"What's going on?" he asked as he pushed his way past one of the bodyguards.

Don Reza waved off his bodyguard and said, "Your friends have offered to assist you with the task I have chosen as your favor. I have the address you require and will release it to you once my matter is resolved."

Yep, the cold, calculating Don knew exactly what he was doing. No address unless he got what he wanted first. Gunner hadn't looked at him and the rock in his stomach was getting heavier by the moment. Conor hadn't ever thought the Don would show up out of the blue before Conor had a chance to explain.

"You have your deal," Brick stated.

"Wonderful." The Don smiled, but you could never be sure if he meant it.

"Wait, what task are you talking about, and why couldn't this have been an email?"

Don Reza snapped his fingers, and one of his bodyguards produced a file, which he placed into Conor's hands.

"All the information you require is in there. As for my visit, you know I prefer the personal touch. And I wanted to see what brought you, of all people, to nowhere Texas."

"It's nothing illegal, right?"

"That was our agreement. You are to do your job as a private investigator, and with your friends' help, completing this task should be no problem."

"But they aren't involved in this. The deal was between you and me."

"Your friends are quite persuasive. I could use them on my payroll."

"Not interested," Brick growled.

Gunner remained silent.

Don Reza grinned. "I suppose not. But I'm a man of my word. Find out what this company is hiding, and you will have the address."

"Why are you interested in this company?" Brick asked.

"That's my business."

Conor didn't miss the flash of anger in Reza's eyes. Someone had pissed off the Don. Never a good idea if you wanted to live a long and healthy life.

"And if we can't find the information you need?" Conor had to ask.

"Then the man you seek remains in hiding."

"We need the location."

"Then I suggest you talk about that with your friends. I'll be in touch."

Don Reza returned to the backseat of his SUV and shut the door. Visit concluded.

The minute the vehicles pulled away from the lake house, Conor lost it. "What the hell are you guys thinking? This favor has nothing to do with any of you. I made the deal. It's on me to repay the debt. There's no way I'm allowing this team to get involved with Don Reza."

Brick looked at him and smiled. "Are you done?"

Conor snapped, "Maybe."

"Come with me," Gunner said, and Conor was powerless to stop himself from following him into the tree line. This wasn't going to be good.

Once they were out of sight Gunner grabbed onto Conor's shirt collar and pushed him back against a large tree. Yep, not good.

"You made a deal with a Don known for his cruelty and murderous rage."

There was no lying about this. "Yeah. No one could find Ben's father, not even Spence."

"And what makes you think the sperm donor wants to help? He took off on them after Ben was born."

"It's a feeling."

"A feeling?" Gunner asked, looking less than convinced.

"Um, yeah." How the hell was he going to explain his unusual talent without looking like a lunatic? "Please, I know it sounds crazy but I just know."

"Risking your life with that Don over a feeling. Yeah, you're fucking insane."

"You have to trust me. We need to find Ben's bio father. He can help stop his parents. Honestly, I never intended to involve the team in this favor, but what's done is done."

"Why didn't you tell me from the start?" Gunner asked while releasing him and turning away.

"I didn't want to give you hope in case I couldn't find the guy."

"You were willing to make a deal with the devil in an attempt to protect Ben from the Wellses?"

"Yep."

"Who else knew about this plan?"

"Obviously Brick, but Spencer figured it out on his own, and, of course, my family. I begged them not to tell you so don't be mad at them. This is on me. I thought Brick told you considering you were with him talking to the Don."

"No. He asked me to back him up when the vehicles pulled in and to stay silent. Don Reza was all too happy to announce he'd found Jason Wells's address as you had bargained for."

"I'm sorry. I should have told you." Shoulda, coulda, woulda, didn't matter now.

Conor didn't know what else to say. He'd fucked up and possibly lost the trust of the man who'd grown to mean so much to him. How had everything gotten so turned around when he'd only wanted to help?

After the night they'd spent together he'd thrown caution to the wind and jumped into this relationship with both feet. Now it might come back and bite him in the ass.

Gunner turned to face him, his expression unreadable. His eyes were drilling into Conor's head as if searching for answers or deceit.

Conor had already given him all he had, but was it enough?

"Come here," Gunner said as he opened his arms, and Conor didn't have to be asked twice. His big arms felt so good wrapped around him. "No more secrets."

"Promise, that's it. I'm sorry, I thought I was doing the right thing."

"I know, but if we're going to make this work, we do it together."

"Agreed."

"Okay, let's go inside and discuss our next steps," Gunner suggested as he released Conor.

"What did Brick say to get Reza to agree to the team's help?" Conor asked as they linked hands and walked back out of the forest.

"Let's just say we know a few people in common," Gunner stated.

"Do I want to know?" Conor asked.

"Not really."

For a second time, the people he cared about were in danger because of him. First, with that damn subpoena, and now with a mobster. The first was his fault. The second, Brick's on behalf of the team.

Knowing that didn't make Conor feel any better.

CHAPTER SIXTEEN

Conor

They'd gone through Reza's file, and the team had constructed a command center in the lake house's living room. Everyone was busy researching an upstate New York company called Brower Inc. to uncover what about it had caught Reza's attention.

So far, they'd learned Brower was owned by a wealthy, influential family originally from Massachusetts. They produced computer CPUs, motherboards, and memory chips for computer systems, and had contracts with many of the top companies across the country.

"Why would Reza care about a computer hardware company?" Conor asked no one in particular.

"That's what we need to find out," Fletch said. "There has to be a good reason this outfit caught the Don's attention."

"Who wants coffee?" Julia asked as she, Matthew, and Ben came over, bearing gifts.

Different types of coffee from Julia's fancy machine, along with plates of crackers, veggies, and cheese, and another with cookies. The boys carried the food while Julia handed out the coffee. Grandma and Aunt Viv were busy making a huge pot of sauce for the cannelloni they were preparing for supper.

"Thank you, guys. We needed this," Conor said.

He took a sip of his vanilla latte and groaned. Julia had that machine figured out, and everyone was happier because of it.

"Uncle Gunner, can I stay at Matthew's cottage tonight?"

They hadn't finished setting up their cottage due to Reza's surprise visit and the ensuing activity once they started going through the file.

"Is it okay with Matthew's mom?" Gunner asked.

"Yes. Julia said to ask you to make sure it's okay."

"Then all I can say is," Gunner teased and made a big show about his decision, "have fun, buddy."

Ben hugged Gunner around the neck and went running back to Matthew.

"He said yes."

The kids were too cute.

"You're sure I can't talk you guys out of this?" Conor couldn't help but try one more time to dissuade the team.

A chorus of "No" followed.

The team had decided he was a member, and when one member had a problem, all members got involved. The feeling of belonging had settled his concerns about fitting in. Especially since he was moving all his worldly possessions to Texas to be with Gunner and Ben.

Conor didn't want the team involved, but he was thankful to have them by his side.

"I put out a few feelers, and Uncle Marty took up surveillance of the building until we can fly back to New York."

"As it relates to the owners, I keep coming up with a recurring theme over the last three years of Les and Becky Brower's lives," Spence told the group.

"And that is?" Shaw asked.

"Politics. It appears the owners have been hosting quite a few senators and governors lately, and there's mention of Les running for a seat in the House of Representatives," Spence continued.

"Can I have that list?" Conor asked.

"It's in your inbox."

"Christ, you're fast."

Conor ran a search on each of the politicians that'd been wined and dined by the Browers. There was a good number on the list, so it took a bit of time, but soon the program he'd designed did its job.

"Okay, a few things these people have in common. Most of them have been lobbied on behalf of big tech companies at various points in their careers. Each has voted in favor of bills benefiting companies like Brower's. From mining precious metals for these systems to receiving government contracts, which led to more private contracts."

"A lot of big companies lobby the government to get special treatment," Brick said. "It's common for people in Congress to get hit up by special interest groups and big corporations."

"Yeah, but we're not looking into those other companies. Reza has something against the Browers and wants us to dig up any dirt we can find."

"Good point. Everything Brower does is under the microscope," Roman stated.

"Is there anything else they have in common?" Gunner asked.

"Hold on," Conor said as he sent out a search and let his program do the work.

"Okay, they're politically motivated. Lots of rich folks are, but there has to be something different about these people," Kyle said from his seat beside Shaw.

The sound of keyboards clicking filled the room as the team searched for every morsel of information they could unearth. The sound was interrupted by the beep on Conor's phone. He took it out of his pocket and tapped the screen.

Looks like Brower is having an after-hours party.

The text message from Uncle Marty had several pictures attached.

"Marty sent over a few pics at Brower's. Something is going on in the building."

Conor shared the snaps with the team. The first picture showed two cube vans backed up to the darkened building time-stamped six pm. In the next picture, men in suits could be seen carrying boxes from an open door to the waiting vans.

There was nothing distinctive about the vans, but the workers wearing suits didn't fit. Most employees left at five pm when the company officially closed its doors for the day, but there was no way of knowing if these guys worked for Brower.

They had to figure out why they were there and what they were doing.

"Ask Marty to follow them. Safely," Brick admonished.

"I'll ask."

Uncle Marty, would it be safe to follow them?

Should be no problem. I'll keep you updated.

"He says he'll do it."

"Good. In the meantime, everyone needs to pack a bag. We leave for the airport at 0600."

"Are we coming?" Ben asked as he linked arms with Matthew.

"No, buddy. Not this time. It's work. But we shouldn't be gone long. You guys get to spend time at the ranch," Gunner said.

"Do we get to ride the ponies?" Matthew asked.

Kyle was quick to say, "For sure, guys. We might even have to ride more than one time."

Ben and Matthew looked at each other, both excited. "We'll go pack our toys." The two took off to the upstairs playroom to gather their much-needed supplies.

Conor would never regret what he did to find Ben's father. The boy's smile and happiness were all the reward he needed.

Conor looked away from the stairs and caught Gunner watching him. His look was unreadable, but this time Conor didn't worry about what that meant. They were in a whole different place now.

***

Gunner

Gunner pulled Conor closer as the stream of hot water from the shower head beat down on his aching shoulders. Gunner was happy they'd decided to splurge on the big walk-in shower. Ben was spending the night with Matthew and Julia, and Gunner and Conor had decided to spend the night in their partially moved-in cottage. A mattress on the floor would have to do for tonight.

Conor wrapped his arms around Gunner's waist and leaned into the soothing water. Their bodies fit together as if made for one another, and Gunner could never get enough of the calming feeling he had around his man. Conor had changed his and Ben's lives for the better.

"I love you, Conor."

His lover's grip tightened, but he remained silent, and since he was looking down, it was impossible for Gunner to read his face.

"I know I'm hard to deal with, I can be an asshole, I have a temper, I'm bossy, and I hate change. But if you give me a chance, I know I can do better."

"You're forgetting," Conor said as he looked up. "Those are the finer qualities that drew me to you."

Conor's smile renewed Gunner's hopes he hadn't made a huge mistake.

"Then you're crazier than me," Gunner joked.

"Crazy in love with you." Conor grinned, and Gunner's heart began beating again.

"Yeah?"

"Yeah."

Gunner didn't wait for another word to be spoken. He took Conor's lips in a scorching kiss that had them both rubbing their wet bodies against one another in search of relief from their aching shafts.

Gunner reached down and brought their hard cocks together in his large hand. Then he began pumping up and down, making their wet cocks to glide together, turning that ache into insane pleasure.

"I've never told anyone outside my family that I loved them," Gunner confessed.

"You won't regret it, babe. I love you as you are. Neither of us is perfect."

"You are, for Ben and me."

"For a man of few words, you certainly know what to say."

Things went from hot to scorching as Gunner continued to stroke their cocks together as the steam rose around them. Their moans echoed off the tiled walls and surrounded them in this indulgent moment.

Gunner couldn't imagine his life without Conor and would do everything in his power never to find out.

"I'm close, babe," Conor groaned.

Gunner increased his pace and brought his other hand down to wrap around the other side of their straining cocks. With the hot water washing over them, Gunner's hands brought them to their release as Conor leaned against him for support.

This was the beginning of his new life, and Conor was the man he chose to create it with.

He couldn't think of anyone more fitting than the man who'd come out of nowhere and shaken up his status quo.

The same man who infuriated him and calmed him. The man who knew what he was capable of and refused to see him as a monster.

The man he loved who loved him.

CHAPTER SEVENTEEN

Conor

The team was in upstate New York. They'd rented a house in the same town in Lenox where the Browers' company was located. The town had a population of roughly nine thousand and seemed nice enough. Uncle Marty was on his way over to brief what he'd learned from the night at Brower when the guys in suits were moving things into vans.

Grandma and Aunt Viv had taken the opportunity to hitch a ride back home to the Jersey shore. Now that Conor knew they weren't at the lake house anymore, he began to miss them. He'd enjoyed having them there no matter how much he groaned about it.

"I have something I think we all should have a look at," Spence said as he walked into the living room.

He opened his computer screen and turned it for all of them to see. It was an article from over four years ago. Les Brower was being interviewed for some society piece, and in it he stated his interest in running for the House of Representatives on a campaign pledge to see Don Reza behind bars.

"The smoking gun," Conor said. "This is why Reza wants to shut down Brower."

"It seems so," Spencer agreed.

There was a knock on the front door, and Gunner went to answer it. Uncle Marty walked into the living room, his usual cigar hanging out of the corner of his mouth, and his fedora in place.

"Uncle Marty," Conor said as he hugged him in welcome. "It's good to see you."

"You too, my boy," Marty said as he slapped Conor on the back. "These here your friends?"

"Yeah." Conor went to stand beside Gunner. "This is Gunner. It's his nephew who's in danger."

"Thank you for helping protect Ben," Gunner said and held out his hand.

"From what I've been told, those Wellses are a real piece of work."

"They are."

"This is Brick, Spence, Fletch, and Shaw. They all own LH Investigations."

After introductions and the handshakes, Uncle Marty got down to business. "There's something strange going on over at Brower."

"What do you mean?"

"I followed those vans back to the Browers' compound outside the city."

"They could've been delivering something completely legal. There's no way to know," Spence said.

"True, but I'm sure you'll be able to figure it out with one of these," Marty said as he pulled out what looked like a complete motherboard. "These were in those boxes."

"How did you manage to get one?" Fletch asked.

"One of the guys had to take a piss, so I lifted it when he was otherwise occupied."

Spence reached over and took the part, looking excited. "I'll tear this apart and have a breakdown of the components by morning."

Their information specialist shut his laptop and retreated to the kitchen's marble island with its excellent lighting.

"How many boxes did they load up?" Brick asked.

"When I looked inside the van, there had to be over twenty boxes with five to six units in each box."

"Wonder why they waited for the normal workers to leave," Shaw said.

"That's what we need to uncover, and I bet that board Marty brought will give us a direction," Brick stated.

"So, we have Reza pissed at Brower for using him as his political platform, but that was years ago. I can't imagine why that would bother him. There has to be a hundred politicians who called him out as a blight on society. Now he wants the dirt on the guy? That doesn't play for me," Gunner said. "And since we're looking, we learn Brower is busy hiding whatever he's doing and is schmoozing with his allies."

"That about sums it up," Shaw said.

"I'm getting a headache," Conor grumbled as he rubbed his temples.

"It's getting late," Brick stated. "We'll have more information in the morning. Get some shut-eye, and we'll pick it up at 0600."

Music to Conor's ears. He was beat and could use a few hours curled up beside Gunner, and that's what they did for the rest of the night.

***

In another part of town.

"Where is it?" His patience was wearing thin.

"I don't know," the buffoon answered.

He'd have to be choosier with the muscle he hired next time. "You were responsible for those boxes, and now one unit is missing."

"I understand, Mr. Brower. We searched around the building, but it didn't turn up."

"If that falls into the wrong hands, everything I've worked for is ruined." He wasn't going to let that happen.

"I'm sorry, Mr. Brower. It won't happen again."

Brower could see the fear in the man's eyes. A thrill worked through his body. "See that it doesn't," Brower growled, and with a look to his right-hand man, Rocko, Brower had assured it never would.

Les Brower shook the dirt from his leather loafers and returned to his waiting car, the sound of a gunshot barely registering as his car pulled away from the waterfront. He had more important concerns to deal with, like explaining why he was short a unit to the buyer.

He didn't need this headache days before announcing his candidacy for a seat in the next state senate elections. Nothing could get in his way. Not now when the finish line was so close. He'd make it without question even if he had to shoot ten meathead guards. They were nothing in the grand scheme of things. Less than nothing.

It was his turn to wield power instead of lobbying for it.

And with his devices in place, it'd be only up from there.

He'd always thought President Brower had a nice ring to it.

CHAPTER EIGHTEEN

Gunner

"He washed up this morning," Marty said as he handed out the picture of a body found in the lake. He made a friend at the police station who kept him in the loop. Uncle Marty was good at making friends wherever he went.

"And you're sure it's the same guy?" Gunner asked.

"Yep. He's the one I swiped the part from the other night. Except for the hole in his head."

"Him being dead leads me to believe someone wasn't happy it got lost," Shaw said as he poured himself a cup of coffee.

"I didn't think they'd kill the guy." Marty shook his head.

Gunner heard the guilt in Marty's voice.

"You didn't kill him. Whoever shot the guy is responsible for their actions," Conor stated. "More than likely, the guy was a hired thug. He knew what world he lived in."

"I guess we're skipping past the assumption of innocence and going straight to dirty as sin at this point?" Shaw raised a brow.

"Yeah," Spence answered as he entered the living room with the part he had been given in multiple pieces on a tray. "Brower is more than dirty. He's a spy."

"What?" Conor asked. "Espionage? How the hell do you know that?"

"Because of this," Spence said while holding up a small piece of the part. "This is no ordinary motherboard and CPU." He shook his head. "I'll save you the technical jargon. This one part is designed to run your computer and copy everything the user does, receives, and creates. Then it transmits the information back to a central hub at scheduled intervals."

"Brower has government contracts," Brick stated.

"Yeah. Several across multiple divisions," Conor said.

"We'll need that list," Brick ordered.

"On it." Conor got busy.

"We need eyes on the Brower building and Les and Becky Brower."

"Got that," Fletch said.

"I need to make a couple of calls," Brick muttered as he grabbed his coffee mug and left the room.

"Holy shit. Do you think they're working for a foreign government? Or terrorists?" Conor asked.

"We can't assume they're not," Gunner answered.

"Reza should be thrilled," Shaw commented before taking a gulp from his mug.

"This leaves Reza in the dust. This is about our country's national security," Fletch said. "I'm going to drive around town and get a lay of the land."

"I'll come with you," Spence said.

"Good idea. I'll get working on that list for Brick," Conor said.

Gunner knew what needed his attention: securing the perimeter. It was apparent these people were willing to kill to protect their secret. He'd make sure no one popped up at their back door. This would likely turn ugly before it was over.

***

Conor

The list read like a who's who in the government and armed forces. Brower had his machines on multiple levels along various chains of command. Conor had a sick feeling in his stomach when he confirmed the Navy was one of them, though he wasn't certain they were used in any of the SEALs units.

How long had Brower been at this? The asshole had to have greased more than one palm to get his equipment this far up the food chain. The potential damage could be extensive, and US military secrets were always up for sale to the highest bidder.

In a weird twist of fate, the Don's favor turned into an honest-to-goodness case. Conor hoped the damage was minimal, but they wouldn't know that until they broke the case and the cleanup began. The sooner they got those systems shut down, the better.

He found Brick in the kitchen brewing yet another pot of coffee. His phone was stuck to his ear, and Conor waited until Brick noticed him. When he did, Conor waved the piece of paper. Brick stopped, looked at the sheet, and nodded without missing a beat of his phone conversation. Conor imagined multitasking was part of Brick's DNA.

Now that his task was completed, Conor went in search of his man. He was still getting used to the concept, especially since he never thought they'd be where they were. Ever.

He walked out the back door to find Gunner on a ladder climbing up to roof. His ass looked phenomenal from this angle.

"What are you doing?" Conor asked.

"Protecting the house."

"By standing on the roof? Shouldn't you at least have a gun?"

Gunner laughed and shook his head. "Smartass. I'm setting up sensors and cameras in case we have any unexpected visitors."

"Oh, that makes more sense," Conor said. "Want some help?"

Gunner slid down the ladder and pulled Conor into his arms.

"Help me with what exactly?" Gunner asked with a suggestive wink.

"Whatever you need," Conor said as he wound his arms around Gunner's neck. He loved seeing the playful side of his lover, which was coming out more often.

Gunner's devilish grin said it all, but before they could continue with that train of thought, a car rolled past the rental way too slowly. The idiots should've a red flashing light on their roof for all their subtleness.

"Who do you think they are?" Conor asked.

"Cops," Brick answered from behind them, but Conor didn't jump. This time, Brick hadn't tried to hide his approach.

"You invite them?" Gunner asked.

"Yep. We need to include them along with the FBI and CIA. This case is bigger than all of us."

"I'm guessing the last two are on their way?" Conor asked.

"They are. We should have a full house by tomorrow morning."

"Great," Gunner growled. "This is going to be a crapshoot."

"Crapshoot?"

"Yeah. It means we could get a helpful, seasoned, professional agent," Brick answered.

"Or we get some punk fresh outta training trying to make a name for himself," Gunner said.

"We'll find out soon enough." Brick nodded.

No matter the situation, the man always looked calm.

"Should we welcome them?" Conor asked.

"Let 'em wait," Gunner said before pulling Conor in for a kiss. Brick chuckled and left the two of them making out by the ladder.

Conor had never thought the day would come when he was free to touch and kiss Gunner whenever he wanted. It felt like having keys to the candy store or, more aptly, the sex shop.

"Tonight can't come fast enough," Conor said.

"Why do we have to wait?"

"Because there are cops in the house."

"So?"

Conor couldn't help but laugh. "And you call me the smartass."

"Call 'em as I see 'em."

"Come on, big guy. Let's say hello," Conor said while taking hold of Gunner's hand and leading him to the back door.

Conor wasn't sure what he expected when they stepped inside, but guns being drawn wasn't on the list. Both he and Gunner pulled their guns and fanned out, aiming at the two men.

"I'm thinking these two aren't the cops."

"They are," Brick stated. "But one of them is a traitor."

"Traitor?" one of the officers asked.

"It was a long time ago," the tall blonde said, but he didn't lower his gun.

"Selling secrets to the scum of the earth doesn't have a time line for absolution, fucktard. You can't be trusted," Brick said, still sounding calm. He hadn't even set down his mug.

The second officer lowered his gun and holstered it. "Put your gun away, Harris."

Harris looked at his partner like he'd lost his mind. "He's still pointing a gun at us."

"Technically, I'm pointing it at you, Harris. Not the officer."

Conor readjusted his aim to Harris as well.

The guy looked around the room. "Listen, I'm not the person I used to be."

"I find that hard to believe." Brick wasn't budging.

"Don't shoot him. He's working as a special consultant on this case," an older man said as he walked into the living room. "The paperwork would be a bitch."

"What the hell you are cooking up, Damini?"

"Put the guns away, for Christ's sake, and I'll tell you."

Brick rolled his shoulders and waited for the Harris guy to lower his weapon. Once he he'd holstered it, Brick nodded, and the three team members lowered their weapons.

"Start talking," Brick ordered.

"It's good to see some things don't change." Damini laughed.

"I will shoot his ass, so make this quick."

Damini took a seat on the couch. "Harris has been working for us for some time now. At least a decade."

"Lemme guess. The hacker works for the cops to keep his ass out of prison." Brick scowled.

"Yeah, Flipper. They made me an offer I couldn't refuse," Harris deadpanned.

"He better be doing righteous work. I caught this POS red-handed auctioning off locations of allied troops and their bases." Brick didn't look so calm anymore, and the Harris dude took a step back. "You hire him *and* give him a fuckin' gun? Not down with that."

"He was seventeen at the time," Damini said.

Conor looked over at the guy who'd done really fucked-up things. He looked normal, except for the tracheotomy scar low on his neck.

"Seventeen or seventy. It makes no difference. He's not trustworthy."

"Yeah, that's what I thought," the officer stated. "I requested reassignment over twelve times."

"And you are?" Conor asked because he hadn't heard his name.

"Devon," he answered.

"Then why are you still partnered with him?" Gunner asked.

Devon glanced at Harris. "He saved my life."

"Don't get all mushy about it." Harris winked.

"See that scar on his neck? Harris took a bullet to the chest protecting me and had been in a coma for almost two months."

"Color me a hero," Harris snarked. "I have no permanent damage other than the scars."

"How did you end up in a situation that called for life-and-death decisions?" Conor asked.

"We were discovered while casing a warehouse in the industrial mall to the south of the city," Harris said. "They had Devon and were about to execute him."

"When Harris came in guns blazing, taking out three guards and the second-in-command. I grabbed a dropped gun and turned to find the head of the snake, but the asshole found me first."

"I saw Devon was in the guy's sights, so I threw my body in front of him. It was gut instinct, so don't get all emotional and shit."

"Harris was hit, but it gave me the opportunity to get a shot off, taking out the kingpin and sending the rest running."

"So, we're supposed to forget all he did to put our military forces in danger because he didn't let Devon die?" Gunner asked.

"Look, all I'm asking is for a chance to prove I've changed," Harris said. "I haven't done anything illegal since," he motioned to Brick, "he caught me."

"Why'd you do it in the first place?" Conor asked.

"I needed the money."

"For what?"

"It doesn't matter anymore."

"It matters to us," Brick said.

It was obvious Harris didn't want to answer.

"You can answer, or you can leave," Brick stated.

Harris lowered his head. "My little sister needed surgery and chemo."

"Where is she now?"

"Dead," Harris answered without looking at them.

Conor looked at Brick, who was staring at Damini, who nodded and said, "It's the truth. We arranged the funeral."

Shit.

"I'm sorry about your sister, but that doesn't forgive what you tried to do," Brick said.

"We can agree he didn't use good judgment in the face of a family emergency." Brick didn't so much as blink, and Damini sighed. "The question is, will you be able to work with him on this case?"

"I'll accept him as a consultant on the case, but one toe crosses the line, and I'll deal with him my way," Brick said.

"Understood." Damini nodded. "But you're doing the paperwork if it goes south."

Conor pointed between Brick and Damini. "How do you know each other?"

"I was an MP back in the day. Now I'm a detective," Damini said.

"Did the team have any run-ins with the MPs?" Conor asked, looking over at Gunner, who grinned.

"Let's just say it's never a good idea to leave a SEALs team with nothing to do," Damini replied.

"C'mon, that latrine wasn't working properly to begin with. We put it out of its misery for the personnel's sake," Gunner said with a straight face.

"To this day, that story circulates through the recruits, and these idiots became an urban legend." Damini shook his head.

Gunner grinned wide, looking damn proud of himself.

CHAPTER NINETEEN

Gunner

Gunner curled his body around his lover. Typically, they spent the night spooning. He wasn't sure how he'd been able to sleep without Conor in his arms, but he never wanted to find out.

The FBI and CIA agents were due in tomorrow. Then they could move forward with taking Les Brower down for his multiple crimes. Becky Brower was an unknown. They hadn't been able to find her name on anything incriminating. Either she was oblivious to her husband's dealings, or they hid her involvement well.

There was no discounting the chance she was kept in the dark and arranged dinner parties since she was his wife. But he wasn't buying it. Even if she didn't know the details, she had to suspect something was up when the who's who of a certain political party darkened their doors.

"Are you sleeping?" Conor whispered.

"No."

"What's keeping you up?"

"Too many unknowns in this case."

"Yeah. Here's hoping we find the answers before Brower and his men find us."

"They wouldn't get within fifty yards of this place."

"Well, that helps me feel better."

"How 'bout I help you feel even better?"

"I like the sound of that," Conor said.

Even though they'd made love before they tried to sleep, Gunner was more than willing to start round two.

Conor rolled over to his back and stared up at Gunner. Conor had no idea how much sway he held over Gunner. It was strange after years of going solo to have someone matter enough for him to change his mind about anything. It'd taken him a while, but he'd finally figured out allowing someone in didn't make him weak. In fact, he was stronger because of it.

He had people he could depend on, which wasn't taken for granted. And a new world was opening up to him. For once, Gunner was ready to explore it.

"What do you have in mind?"

Before Gunner could answer, his telephone pinged and flashed red.

"We have company."

"How rude," Conor said as he rolled out of bed, pulled on his shorts, and grabbed his gun.

Gunner was doing the same, and they began communicating with hand signals before opening the bedroom door. The hall was clear. The other bedroom doors opened, indicating the rest of the team had received the same warning. The police had left over six hours ago, and no one was due to arrive until later this morning.

Brick gave the order to move out, and the team scattered throughout the house. A few went out bedroom windows and took the outside. That's where Gunner and Conor were, moving through the thick hedge around the back of the house.

Conor was on Gunner's six as they moved without sound or light. In all his years as a SEAL, no man could've gone from being his lover to full-out combat mode in a blink of an eye.

They froze when they heard the crack of a fallen branch Gunner had left lying in the yard for that very reason. No one on their team would be that careless. The unannounced visitor had made his second mistake.

There was a small hiss of pain, and Gunner knew exactly where the intruder was. Near the large rose bushes in the back southwest corner of the yard. They moved out as a unit and were joined by Fletch.

They flowed through the trees and bushes, and Gunner was impressed that Conor was keeping pace. He'd never formally trained with them or had been in the military, and still he moved with them like they'd been doing this together for years.

Within moments the three had the intruder surrounded.

"Stop where you are." Whoever it was froze.

"Get down on the ground," Gunner ordered.

The intruder complied, and Conor quickly zip-tied their hands behind their back and searched for a weapon. "No weapon."

"Who do we have here?" Fletch said as he rolled them over and removed their hoody.

"What the fuck?" Gunner growled.

"Harris?"

***

Conor

Conor wasn't sure he was seeing what he was seeing. "What the hell is he doing here?"

"Let's get him inside where we can ask him," Gunner said as he lifted Harris to his feet.

Shaw and Spencer joined them as they brought the guy through the patio doors and into the kitchen, where the drapes had been drawn. Gunner shoved Harris into a waiting chair.

Brick stood at the counter pouring water into the coffee machine. "Once a traitor, always a traitor," Brick said in an icy voice.

"That's not why I'm here," Harris growled.

Brick spun around and stared Harris down until the man was forced to look away. "Why are you here at one in the damn morning sneaking in at the back of the property? If you were legit, you would've come through the front door.

"Damini isn't who you think he is," Harris said in a rush.

"You're going to have to do better than that," Brick stated.

"It's the truth."

"Then who's the real Damini?"

"Do you think I'd come here knowing how much you want me dead if it wasn't real? I need you to believe me."

Conor stepped forward, and surprisingly Brick stepped back. The team was watching Conor closely, so he had to make this work.

One time during an investigation roughly five years ago, Conor touched something and saw strange things. His grams called it his gift, but he didn't discuss it much.

Conor looked at Gunner. "I'm getting the same feeling I do about Jason. The need to find the truth and knowing it's the right thing to do."

"But Harris can't be trusted," Gunner said.

"For all we know, neither can Jason," Conor stated.

"What else are you getting from Harris?" Brick asked.

"He's scared."

"I'm not scared of nothin'," Harris argued.

"That's a lie," Conor huffed, then a flash of something at the very edge of his consciousness caught his attention. "Your sister's alive?"

"What the hell?" Spence said.

That got Harris's attention, and he spoke directly to Conor. "Yeah, she is."

"They took her," Conor stated.

"To keep me under wraps," Harris responded.

"That's what you meant by them making you an offer you couldn't refuse."

"They'd give her the care she needed in return for my working for them."

"Do you know where she is?"

"No. Only that she's alive."

"Why'd you come here?"

"I overheard Damini talking on his phone discussing what you found and who was involved."

"That sounds normal for a detective if he's talking to his supervisor."

"But it wasn't his supervisor."

"Who was it, then?"

"Someone named Rocko."

"Rocko's Les Brower's bodyguard," Spence said.

"Yeah, that's what Damini said, then he gave Rocko this address."

"It's time to bug out," Brick announced. "Five minutes. Harris stays with me."

Fluidly and rapidly, in what seemed like a choreographed movements, they grabbed their gear, stuffed them into their bags, helped get all the physical evidence they'd acquired, and went to the waiting SUVs.

Brick sat in the driver's seat of the first vehicle with Harris in the passenger seat, his hands still behind his back but at least he had his seatbelt on. Fletch took the driver's seat of the second SUV as Conor and Gunner jumped into the vehicle with Brick. Shaw and Spence went in the second SUV.

They pulled away from the rental and hit the highway four minutes and twenty-six seconds later. Spence was already searching out a new location for them to hunker down while they figured this out.

"Why did you risk it all for us?" Conor asked Harris.

"I'm not some heartless bastard. I agreed to help them and believed I was paying off my debt to society by working with the cops to bring the bad guys to justice. But there's no way I'll sit back and watch this happen. I never claimed to be anything but what I was, while Damini is using his position to do much worse, and it's not to help a family member."

"What about your sister?" Gunner asked.

"Well, I hope you'll help me with that. You know, finding her and getting her to safety."

Gunner met Brick's gaze in the rearview mirror. Before he could say anything, his cell rang. "Whatcha got?" he asked. "Right."

"Spencer secured a cabin. Here's the address," Gunner said as he handed his phone over to Brick.

"Got it," Brick said. "We'll scope out the area first."

"Understood."

Conor reached over and took hold of Gunner's hand and squeezed, likely recognizing the corollary between Harris's situation and Gunner's with Ben.

CHAPTER TWENTY

Gunner

Hours later, the team sat around the dining table of their new digs. It was a nice place on a beautiful, wooded property, but they weren't there to relax.

Brick had removed Harris's restraints and had him searched to make sure he wasn't mic'ed, bugged, chipped, or hiding a weapon on his body. Nothing turned up, and he was allowed to remain free, but under constant supervision.

"You guys gotta see this," Spence said as he set down his laptop and hit a few buttons.

The cameras they'd left live at the rental house detected movement, and the screen split into eight different camera views. Gunner watched as figures emerged from the backyard next to theirs and spread out around the rental. Gunner estimated at least twenty individuals had surrounded the house.

Moments later, flames erupted as Molotov cocktails were thrown through the windows and onto the roof. The figures pulled out their guns and waited for the first person to emerge from the burning building. He wasn't surprised by how quickly the building lit up: old construction, mostly made of wood.

They all watched as cameras inside the house documented the flames as they tore through the place. Gunner couldn't help but pull Conor closer. Gunner wasn't so sure all of them would've made it out.

Vehicles pulled up once the building was fully engulfed, and the last thing the cameras recorded was one of the men removing his balaclava from over his face.

"Motherfucker," Brick growled.

Damini's face was screwed up in anger. Then the screens went dead one by one as the cameras melted in the flames.

No one moved for a few beats. Everyone had to be processing what they'd seen. That could've been the end of them.

Brick was the first to move, and soon everyone was seated in chairs staring at the table. Even they, a team trained to do the most dangerous missions in the world, had to take a minute knowing how close they'd come to death. When mortality comes slamming home, even a badass has to take a moment.

Brick cleared his throat. "I'd like to personally thank Harris for doing the right thing. And Conor, who, not for the first time, helped us see beyond what was in front of us."

***

Conor

Brick was back on the phone with who knew who. He had more contacts than the five past presidents combined. Conor hoped it was someone who could help figure a way out of this mess.

Now, they hunted, and they didn't have time to regroup. Ben's hearing was eleven days away, and Conor still didn't have Jason's contact information. Fuckin' Reza.

While Brower may have the high ground, it was a temporary win. His days were numbered, and after this stunt, if the asshole didn't know it, he'd learn soon enough.

Spencer was busy talking with Harris while Fletch and Shaw were on patrol.

Conor and Gunner went through four local drive-throughs so they wouldn't look conspicuous getting enough food to feed the 2nd Fleet. Since they didn't know if they were going to stay at the cabin, shopping for food wasn't necessary, and could potentially put them in more danger. Supermarkets and mom-and-pop stores had cameras. Any of these guys would stand out while buying food. They weren't exactly the kind of men who blended in.

"How are you?" Gunner asked as he dumped all the fast-food bags on the counter.

"I'm good."

"Try again," Gunner said, which had Conor looking up at him.

"It's been a hard day. It has for all of us."

"Yeah, but right now, I'm talking about you."

"Actually," Conor said, "I'm worried about you. This op became high pressure almost from the get-go, and now things have gone south. We can't fail here for more than the obvious reasons."

"Ben," Gunner muttered.

"Yeah, Ben." Conor sighed. "I know we have to stay focused so we can get Jason's information, and then beat those asshole in-laws in court, but I can't pretend I'm not concerned."

"I'm not asking you to pretend. Best we can do is our best. If any group of people can take down Bower and kick in-laws' ass, it's this team. I've trusted my life to these guys more times than I can count. I have to believe they're not going to let me down."

"Us," Conor said. "Not going to let us down."

After the team had stuffed down all the food in all the bags, Spence moved next to Conor and said, "Hey. Can I ask you a question?"

"Sure."

"How much do you know about your parents?"

That caught Conor off guard, considering he'd been thinking about them a lot lately.

"Next to nothing. I was dropped off at the orphanage, and they never looked back. Why?"

"Before we started this op, I'd been researching a time line relating to the Noah Project and your appearance at the orphanage came up."

"The Noah Project? The last case you guys worked on with the genetically modified kids?"

"Yeah. I could be off base, but I wondered if you might be one of the missing kids, and that's how you came about your...gift. You know, how you know what people are feeling and if they're telling the truth."

"So you're saying I'm not only weird, but a genetically modified weirdo." Great. After a life filled with unanswered questions, he might be a spliced-together test-tube baby.

"What's going on?" Gunner was by his side before Conor realized it.

"I'm sorry, but Ben and Harris's sister are at the forefront of my mind, and I got to thinking about the Noah Project and what might be a connection to you. I wanted you to know there's a possibility." Spence continued by saying, "You were left at an orphanage not far from the location of one of the Noah Project facilities. You have this gift, but no answers as to why. Your age lines up with one of the facilities' known operating periods."

Gunner's arm wrapped around Conor's shoulders.

"I guess it might answer a question," Conor mumbled.

"What question, *milacek*?"

"Why?"

"I don't know, but when we're done with this and Ben's deal, I'm going to look into it more."

"Okay," Conor said, not knowing what else he could say.

"Anyway," Spence raised his voice, "what I wanted to tell everyone is Harris and I have an idea."

Brick crumpled his bag, and then said, "Let's hear it."

"We think we could create a program that would have a dual effect on Brower's system," Spencer said. Brick made a keep-going motion with his hand.

"If we can load it onto a computer that has one of Brower's motherboards attached, we believe we can erase all the stolen information that hasn't been moved out of the connected files," Harris said.

"And at the same time, the program will report back any information we find on their end," Spencer concluded.

That sounded amazing, but where would they find a computer with the motherboard attached?

"We must find an entry point to get the program in," Shaw said what Conor was thinking.

"Are we going to break into a senator's house?" Conor had an idea. "Do you still have the stuff Marty lifted that day?"

"Yeah, but it's still in pieces," Spence said.

"There's a computer in the office upstairs. It has a tower. Can you put the pieces back together and install the new part to that computer to connect to their system?" Conor suggested, not knowing enough about computers to know if it could work.

"I'll have to check the computer," Spence said.

Harris stood and tossed his bag, then headed for the stairs.

"Where are you going?" Spence asked.

"To check out the computer."

Spence joined him.

Brick stared at the empty stairway. It would take a lot for Brick to trust Harris. Conor bet Brick was torn between how he felt about Harris and the need to get the job done so they could move on securing Jason and making the in-laws and their bullshit custody hearing a thing of the past.

***

Gunner was on the phone with Ben while Conor read over the text he'd received from Don Reza.

Hear things are heating up for Brower. Good work.

Fuckin' Reza. He knew he'd jammed them up, and gotten away with it because of Ben. What a fucker. And while it seemed Brower was one hundred times worse than the Don, nothing would stop them from getting to the bottom of this shit in record time.

A little boy's—and Harris's sister's—lives were on the line.

CHAPTER TWENTY-ONE

Brower

"I can't return to my home or my life," Damini yelled over the phone, causing Brower to pull it away from his ear. "I've been outed for taking bribes."

"If you'd done your job, this wouldn't be a problem," Brower shot back. This joker was dancing on his last nerve. "Have you told the authorities anything?"

"No. I need to get out of the country," Damini growled, sounding ready to snap.

"Then go." Why was the disgraced detective bothering him about this?

"I haven't got those resources, but you do," Damini hissed.

"You want me to get you out of the country?" Seriously. This guy was a tool. Nothing more.

"Yeah. And if you don't get me to South America, I'll start singing like a canary," he threatened.

Why were people so predictable?

"Fine. I'll have Rocko drive you to my private airfield."

"Good. I knew you'd see it my way."

Disappointing to learn the detective had always been this dim-witted.

"Text Rocko with the address. Everything will be handled."

"The sooner, the better."

"On that, we agree. Good-bye, Damini."

Brower ended the call, and moments later, Rocko's phone pinged.

"Got him," Rocko stated.

"Good. Make it look like he killed himself. The guilt of what he'd done too much to continue, or some shit like that. While you're at it, line his pockets with whatever drug you choose as added assurance that his word was unreliable in case he leaves information behind."

"It'll be done."

"Good."

When Rocko didn't walk away, Brower said, "Yes?"

"What do you want to do about the SEALs?"

"I'm sure those boys are on their way back to whatever they do in Texas. They won't be bothering us anymore."

Who did they think they were coming to his town and attempting to put him out of business? Brower was confident the ashes of their rental were enough to have them running scared.

***

Gunner

Gunner looked at the picture on the screen from today's local news. Another body had turned up over in the river. Damini.

"Looks like Brower is getting rid of his lackeys," Shaw said from over his shoulder.

"They're saying it was a suicide." Gunner shook his head. "Yeah, right."

"Couldn't have happened to a nicer guy," Fletch said. "Though I would've liked to get some answers from him first."

"Whatever he knew has gone to the grave with him," Conor said. "Now what?"

"Now, we break into Brower's offices," Brick said as he, Spencer, and Harris entered the dining room. They didn't look happy.

Gunner said, "I take it we can't use the computer in the house to get your program on Brower's servers."

"Correct," Brick stated.

"Damn, that sucks." Shaw said what they all were thinking. "We'll need the schematics of the building."

"Done." Spencer held up his laptop.

"We need a game plan," Conor said. "I'm sure the place is heavily guarded."

Fletch nodded. "Probably even heavier now."

"That's why we're SEALs," Brick stated. "All in, all the time. Now let's get this done to protect our country."

"Yes, sir," the team said.

***

Conor

The team worked all day and well into the night going over their plans until they were imprinted on each of their brains. Tomorrow night they'd go in, and would get out without anyone being the wiser.

Spencer and Harris would access the systems remotely and take control of the cameras, security, and all the facilities within and around the building. Once they'd done that, Fletch and Shaw would secure the exterior while Brick, Conor, and Gunner went in to download the program saved on the thumb drive in his pocket. Conor's job was to get to the nearest computer and upload the program. If everything worked, the information would be sent back to Spencer.

They all had to be ghosts.

The team had less than twenty-four hours before the mission commenced, and Conor and Gunner were taking time to FaceTime with Ben, as well as doing other things to keep them level.

"Yesss, that's it," Gunner moaned, making Conor feel ten feet tall.

He knew Gunner didn't bottom often and wanted to make sure his mind was blown. To that end, Conor made sure he brushed the head of his cock against his lover's prostate with every thrust.

The feeling of having his strong, stoic lover writhing in pleasure underneath him was intoxicating. Conor couldn't stop himself from running his palms across Gunner's broad chest and pushing his fingers into Gunner's dark chest hair.

"You are drop-dead gorgeous," Conor growled before taking Gunner's lips in a heat-filled kiss. "Inside and out."

"You bring it out in me." Gunner grinned before grabbing hold of Conor's waist and increasing the pace.

"Even when you're bottoming, you're not bottoming." Conor laughed.

"Are you surprised?"

"Not really."

Conor sped up as requested and dove into Gunner's tight, wet hole. He could feel his balls pull up tight, but there was no way he'd come before Gunner. Conor wrapped his hand around Gunner's hard cock and began pumping in time with his thrusts.

Gunner's big arms flew out to his sides as he dug his fingers into the sheets. The sound of ripping fabric filled the air, driving Conor to new heights.

"Close," Gunner growled a moment before his hole clamped down on Conor's cock, and he exploded across his muscled abs.

Conor managed to thrust one more time before he came with a deep groan and collapsed onto Gunner. His heart was racing in his chest as he tried to control his breathing. His man was going to kill him with mind-blowing sex.

He couldn't help but chuckle at that thought.

"What?"

"I was wondering if you could die by amazing sex."

The bed started moving as Gunner laughed. "What a way to go."

CHAPTER TWENTY-TWO

Gunner

The darkened Brower building looked innocuous enough, but they knew the truth about what lay within. Gunner couldn't help but wonder how many employees knew what was being made there. Even the people who created some of the parts might not know what they did.

Often in outfits like this, the work was siloed intentionally so no one group knew exactly why they were manufacturing what they were manufacturing. And when put together, the workers on the assembly line wouldn't have any knowledge about what was in the component parts.

This was the same method employed on the Manhattan Project. People worked on separate parts of what would eventually create the atomic bomb, but they had no idea what they were working on.

"In place," Shaw said, his voice carried by their bone mics attached behind their ears. They were dependable and picked up even the softest voices, freeing their ears to detect any nearby movement.

"Same," Fletch reported.

Conor looked over at Brick, waiting for the signal as they crouched behind a delivery truck.

"Five, four," Spencer began counting down, "three, two, we have control of their systems."

"Move out," Brick ordered, and they were off into the dark.

Gunner's heart clenched as he watched his lover take off, but he had to keep his head in the game. No distractions. Conor would be fine. He could handle himself.

They would all be fine. They had to be. They needed to get this muthafucka done so they could move on to tracking down Jason and beating the shit out of the in-laws in court. Then there was the matter of Harris's sister.

Shut it down.

The three of them made it to the entry point and quickly unscrewed the large vent cover. They climbed into the ventilation shaft, replaced the cover, and went into the building's service areas. They should be six rooms away from the reception desk's computer.

Brick pointed up, and Gunner went in search of higher ground where he could keep an eye on this section of the first floor while Conor and Brick moved out.

Gunner slipped his rifle onto his back and used a four-drawer filing cabinet to reach the exposed ceiling. It was one of those modern concepts with the ceiling joists visible but painted black, while the office walls were beige.

When he found the best position to see most of the floor, he hunkered down and lined up his sight.

"In place," he said as he watched Brick lead the way down the hall with Conor taking his six to make sure no one snuck up on them.

The floor looked empty, but they knew there were six guards on duty, four on the inside and two on the exterior. The building had four floors, so the odds of at least one guard patrolling on this floor were high.

"On the move," Fletch said. Alerting them that one of the exterior guards was moving. "East end, smoke break."

Gunner watched Brick motion for Conor to head for the reception area while Brick covered him. Gunner took a deep breath and let the world melt away as his concentration took over and he homed in on his target.

This time, he'd protect instead of eliminate.

The love of his life was down there, and he'd be damned if he didn't cover him.

***

Conor

Each step was measured as Conor crossed the open area between the hallway and the desk. The desk swooped from one side like a giant wave. "Brower" was painted onto the wall behind the desk in thick, gold lettering in case anyone forgot where they were. Next to the company name was a large framed portrait of Les Brower. Pompous asshole.

Get your head on straight, Conor chastised himself. With one final scan of his surroundings, Conor ran the ten feet and jumped behind the desk without making a sound.

"I'm there," Conor whispered.

Conor couldn't see Brick, but he knew he was nearby, and was sure Gunner had eyes on him, making him feel a whole lot calmer. They wouldn't allow anyone to get near him.

"Is the computer on?" Harris asked.

Conor moved the mouse on the desktop bringing the monitor to life. "Yeah."

"Okay. Put the thumb drive in the machine and go to settings," Harris instructed.

"Done." He knew how to operate a computer, but Conor wanted to ensure it was done right. They didn't have any margin for error here.

"Open the drive and download the program. It's password protected: A J Five Eight Nine."

Conor clicked the mouse, entered the password in the box, and opened the file.

"It's downloading."

"It should take thirty seconds at most," Harris assured him.

Conor watched the flashing lights, willing them to move faster. He was starting to feel strange, like his skin was crawling, but he ignored it, and soon enough, the download was complete, and he removed the thumb drive.

"Done."

"Good. Let's get out of here," Brick ordered.

Conor couldn't ignore the growing feeling. "Something's not right."

"What is it?" Brick asked.

"I don't know, but everything inside me tells me not to move."

Then the sound of a door opening broke the near silence. Someone was coming their way.

"We've got company," Gunner said.

Maybe that's what he was feeling, the guard getting closer. All three froze in place as the footsteps came from Conor's right. He heard the guard's radio crackle as other guards checked in.

"Frank here. I'm doing rounds on the first floor, over."

Great, now what?

"We need a distraction," Brick whispered through the connection.

"On it," Spence said.

The guard walked around the front of the desk, mere feet away from where Conor was hiding. He had his Glock at the ready if things went south and he had to fight his way out. He *so* didn't want to do that.

"Easy, *milacek*." Gunner's voice flowed through him. Its calming effect instantaneous.

"Got your distraction, be ready to move," Spence said.

A few moments later, he heard a lot of water gushing through the pipes in the ceiling. Then the guard's radio lit up.

"The toilets are backing up on the second floor. I need help," a guard yelled over the radio.

"On my way," Frank, the guard, replied. Conor listened as Frank's boots sounded, running in the opposite direction of where they needed to go.

"Nice, Spence," Conor said.

Conor crawled from underneath the desk and quickly joined Brick in the hallway. When they made it back to the service area, they met up with Gunner before climbing out through the ventilation shaft and resealing the cover.

Fletch and Shaw were waiting for them to provide cover as they ran to the meetup location, loaded up, and sped away from the Brower building.

Gunner pulled Conor into his arms and held him tight as their SUV pulled onto the nearest interstate.

"Good job, everyone," Brick said. "It was a clean exit."

"I particularly liked the distraction." Conor laughed.

"That should keep them occupied for a while," Gunner said as he rubbed his stubbled chin against the top of Conor's head.

Spence was busy on his laptop, and Conor had to ask. "Did it work?"

"We'll know shortly," Spence said, and the team quieted as they waited.

If it didn't work, they went through all that for nothing, and there was no plan B. Brick had contacts waiting for the information on their end, and they didn't want to leave them hanging.

If the program worked, it'd be the only way to shut Brower and his cronies down for good. Some agencies had already stopped using Brower's systems as a precaution until they had proof the threat was real.

"We're getting something," Spence muttered.

"What?" Fletch asked.

"Hold on," Spence said.

"Come on, please work," Conor begged. He wanted all this to be over so he could find Jason, Gunner could return to Ben, and they could kick ass at the custody hearing.

"Yesss," Spence shouted.

"It's working?" Brick asked.

"Yeah, it is," Spence said. "We're receiving a shitload of information on Brower and his associates."

Harris looked proud. Conor had to feel for the guy. Life hadn't been easy. Sure, he'd made some bad choices for good reasons, but he'd always walk with the shadow of his betrayal. Before they finished this op, they'd have to find his sister.

"Are there more people involved?" Fletch asked.

"Foreign powers interested in what Brower has to offer," Harris said.

Spence snarled. "Soon, there won't be anything once we shut him down."

"Damn right," Gunner agreed.

"I hate to break up the celebrations, but we've got a tail," Shaw announced from the driver's seat.

Everyone went on alert as Brick took a look through his side mirror. "The silver Dodge?"

"That's the one. We picked him up a few off-ramps back. He's changing lanes with us and hasn't used his turn signals once."

"License plate?" Harris asked as he opened his laptop. The guy was fast.

"New York," Gunner said, and told him the plate number.

"Let's see who you are," Harris said as he typed. "Bingo."

"Who's it registered to?" Brick asked.

"Devon Brown. Shit."

"Isn't that your old partner?" Fletch asked.

"Yeah, it is," Harris answered, but Conor could feel there was more to it.

"I forgot about that guy," Fletch said.

"Is he dirty?" Brick asked.

"I don't think so, but I don't know for sure. He and Damini weren't friends or anything. The last time I saw him was when I was heading out," Harris said.

"The night you came to our first rental?" Brick asked.

"Yeah. He was on his way home."

"Well, let's find out how invested he is," Brick said with a nod to Shaw.

"Hang on." Shaw laughed before flooring the SUV. The crazy bastard sped up, crossed three lanes, and took the next off-ramp.

Conor turned in his seat to keep an eye on their tail. Traffic was slow at this hour, so there was low danger of involving a civilian vehicle. Devon's car kept up with them and made the off-ramp to continue with the pursuit.

"I found Damini's name in one of Brower's files," Spence announced as he read the laptop screen, "but I can't find anything on Devon Brown."

"Maybe he's clean," Harris said. "I never saw him do anything questionable."

"Then why is he following us?" Shaw asked.

"Maybe he wants answers like we do," Conor said.

Brick looked at Conor. "Is that what you feel?" Amazing how quickly his gift had been accepted as legitimate information.

Conor dug deep but came up empty. "Nothing. I'm getting nothing."

"Maybe he needs to be closer," Fletch suggested.

"Okay, let's find a nice, secluded place for a conversation," Brick ordered. "And then Conor can have his chance."

A couple of minutes later, Shaw pulled into the parking lot of an old, run-down building with plenty of trees. He spun the SUV around to face Devon's oncoming car, and the team jumped out fully armed, ready for battle.

Devon stopped his car several yards back, perhaps having second thoughts. Conor knew he would be if faced with the team. They spread out, and Conor moved closer to Devon's car in case he could catch a stray emotion or thought from the officer.

From where he was standing, Conor could confirm it was indeed Devon driving. But it wasn't until Harris stepped out of the SUV that Devon turned off his ignition and stepped out with his hands up.

Now that the guy was out of his car, Conor could feel the confusion and anger rolling off the man. This gift wasn't predictable. Sometimes Conor could feel something thousands of miles away, and the next he had to get within twenty feet.

"Confusion and anger," Conor announced, keeping the team up to speed.

Brick nodded. "Why are you following us, Devon?"

"To get some answers," he said.

"What's your question?" Brick asked.

"My question? Hell, I show up for work the morning after meeting you, and Harris is missing, and then Damini turns out to be a dirty cop and washes up dead in the river with two speedballs in his pocket.

"Your rental is burnt to the ground, and everything I thought I knew might not be real. Then the PD dropped the case, stating another department had taken it over. Yeah, I have questions. I have a whole lot of damn questions. I thought we were partners, Harris. I thought I could trust you with anything. What the fuck is going on here?"

"I'm sorry, man," Harris said. "It's better if you stay out of this. It's dangerous."

Conor understood where the anger was coming from. Devon was pissed at Harris for taking off without a word. If he were Devon and this shit started happening around him, he'd want to know what was happening.

"What do you know about Damini and Brower?" Brick asked.

"Are they connected?" Devon asked instead of answering.

"That's not going to work with me. Answer the question," Brick ordered.

"I knew nothing about them being connected until right now," Devon stated.

"How long have you worked under Damini?" Brick continued.

"Seven years. He was transferred from another precinct."

"And you never suspected anything was off?" Brick asked.

"Damini and I didn't see eye to eye on a lot of things. We weren't close. I did my job, and I went home."

Conor could feel the rightness of that answer. "He's telling the truth."

Devon looked over at him. "Thanks, but what's his deal?"

"It might be best for you to remove yourself from this case," Brick stated, giving the guy an out and still not answering his question.

"Not a chance. People have to answer for their crimes, and there's no way I'm allowing a possible military breach to go unanswered."

"People have the habit of dying around Brower," Brick stated.

"I've noticed."

Brick seemed to be sizing Devon up, and Devon was doing the same. They were alike in many ways.

"He's Army," Conor said out of nowhere. The word splashed across his mind, and he was sure of it.

"What of it?" Devon growled. "What is wrong with you, man?"

Gunner took two steps forward. "Do not disrespect him."

Devon's hands raised a bit higher into the air. "Got it. Sorry."

"Were you in the Army?" Brick asked.

"Yeah."

"Spence?"

Spencer grabbed his laptop and began doing what he did best: dig. They hadn't had a chance to check out Devon's bona fides, and didn't have a reason to before now.

"Eleven years' worth. Silver Star and Purple Heart recipient retired eight years ago. Two incidents of questioning orders, and one of sneaking off base. Other than those, he's clean."

"How the hell did you get into my file?" Devon asked.

"That's not your biggest worry right now," Spencer said. "But let's just say, I have my ways."

"Ooo, all mysterious and shit." Shaw laughed. "You trying out for the FBI?"

"Fuck off." Spencer laughed and closed his laptop.

Devon looked at them closely. "You guys are special forces. I'm aware of that, but I was told you were all retired."

"Retirement is a fluid concept," Brick said with a grin.

"You're working for the government on this case," Devon stated.

"We are," Brick said, surprising Conor by telling the truth.

"And Harris?" Devon asked. "Back at your rental, you were ready to shoot him. You appeared to hate him and seemed to be buddies with Damini."

"Harris saved our lives the night the rental was torched. As for Damini, we were acquaintances from years ago."

"Can I put my arms down?" Devon asked.

"Are you armed?" Brick asked.

"Of course I am. Shoulder holster left side."

Fletch moved forward, opened Devon's jacket, and removed his service revolver.

"Now you can put your hands down."

Devon let his arms fall to his sides. "When the brass said the case had been taken over, they meant you guys?"

"Yeah. At first, we wanted to include the local authorities, but you know how that turned out," Brick said with a snarl.

"Understandable. You're planning on taking Brower down."

"Yeah."

"Do you need any help?" Devon offered.

"Honest offer," Conor stated.

"Okay, please tell me what's going on with him," Devon said as he pointed at Conor. "Is he all right?"

"His name is Conor. He's part of this team and he's the only reason you're standing here. Keep that in mind," Brick stated. "If we require your assistance, we know how to contact you."

"Okay. Call me anytime, day or night, and I'll be there."

"Stop tailing us," Shaw ordered.

"Got it."

Devon looked over at Harris and asked, "You're safe, man?"

Conor felt the emotion behind that, and it was far more than simply being partners.

"Yeah. I wanna do the right thing," Harris said.

"I know you do," Devon said. "Be careful, okay?"

"You too."

"Move out," Brick ordered, and short minutes later, they were back on the interstate heading to their rental cabin. Devon was probably still picking up his bullets off the pavement from his emptied gun.

CHAPTER TWENTY-THREE

Brower

Brower looked at the numbers again, thinking he'd miscalculated, but he hadn't.

"Explain," he growled.

"Mr. Brower, sir, the flow of information has decreased by over seventy-five percent in the last two days," one of his staff said. He couldn't remember his name, but it didn't matter.

"Why? What's broken?" he demanded.

"Nothing's broken, sir. It seems people are no longer using the systems."

This wasn't happening. He had a meeting with potential clients in less than seventy-two hours.

"Check again," he ordered.

"Sir, I've checked it over a dozen times. The system is working as designed."

"CHECK. IT. AGAIN." He didn't need this idiot questioning his orders.

"Yes, sir."

The man running from the room did help calm his anger a bit, but it didn't last long.

"Rocko, I have a job for you."

***

Gunner

He held Conor tighter, wishing the sunrise would hold off so he could stay with his lover. It'd been a crazy couple of days since they'd broken into Brower's. The information they'd received from the company servers was extensive, and the higher-ups were already taking action to stop the leaks.

The powers that be hadn't moved on arresting the Browers because they received a tip that Les Brower was meeting with clients and they wanted to take down both parties. Of course, they'd be going back in and assisting on the capture along with their FBI counterparts when all he wanted was for that asshole Reza to give Conor Jason's contact information, and more than anything, Gunner wanted to go home to Ben.

"Please tell me you got some sleep," Conor said as he rolled over to face Gunner.

"I think a solid four or so."

"That's better than I'd hoped."

"I wish Reza would give you Jason's info, and after you find him, we can go home and finish this shit."

"Yeah, me too. Soon. After tonight. This should be over."

"I never thought doing a favor for a Don would turn into protecting the country and the men and women in the military. It's like things line up for you somehow."

Conor huffed. "How do you see that?"

"I don't mean you get everything your way, but the connections lead to better things. For example, if you hadn't taken the job with Wells, we wouldn't't've had an honest person helping us keep custody of Ben. You made a deal with Don Reza to find Jason, and if you hadn't, we wouldn't't've been alerted to what was going on at Brower's, and had gotten a chance to stop him. Then Reza gonna hook us up with Jason, and we're going to kick ass in court. No way I'm not going to keep Ben."

"I guess that's one way to see it."

"It's the only way."

Conor's expression changed. He looked...distressed. "Do you think I may be one of those Noah Project kids?"

"I do. The time line fits, but we can't be sure until we find the evidence. We're still working through all the information we've uncovered, and locating all the missing children is more difficult than we expected."

"Then, in reality, I don't have parents, only donors."

Gunner rolled on top of Conor. "You have parents. We need to uncover who they are. This doesn't change anything. I love you, and Ben loves you. That's what matters, the here and now. We'll be great parents."

"I guess."

"Guess?" Gunner asked, grabbing Conor's ass and squeezing. "You can do better than that."

"Okay. I give, but don't stop what you're doing."

"Knew you'd see it my way." Gunner gave Conor's ass a slap. "Now let's take a shower. But first, I have something for you."

"What?"

Gunner rolled over, pulled his surprise from the night table, and handed it to Conor, who held up the chain and read the information on one of Gunner's black dog tags. He'd removed one of his two from around his neck, so his lover could wear it.

Conor was quiet.

"Now if you get lost, they know who to return you to," Gunner joked, trying to lighten the mood.

Conor looked at him through glassy eyes and said, "Thank you. This means the world to me."

Gunner took the chain and placed it over Conor's head. It looked right, hanging around his lover's neck.

"I love you."

"I love you too."

"Good, now let's take that shower." Gunner stood.

"You know I like seeing you in your naked glory, but those windows are pretty big."

"If they wanna look, they can look. But nobody's touching me but you, *milacek*."

"Damn right," Conor said as he slapped Gunner's ass so hard, it left a handprint on his right butt cheek.

***

Conor

Conor was in the last place he wanted to be, outside Brower's office building. Several vehicles were parked out front even though it was ten at night. Eleven FBI agents had joined them for the raid. Unlike last time, Gunner was nowhere near him. Instead, the big guy was positioned on top of a nearby building with his sniper rifle aimed at Brower's office.

Gunner had reported six men and one woman in the meeting with Brower on the third floor while guards were positioned throughout the property. They'd already incapacitated two who had wandered too close to them.

"Two minutes," Brick announced.

Conor took a deep breath and rechecked his gear. It had to be said: he'd never carried so many weapons at once. Gunner had gone overboard with placing a knife at his waist and another in his boot, two handguns were strapped to his thighs, an M4 rifle was in his hands, plus there were throwing knives in a holder strapped across his chest and in the cuffs of his jacket. Gunner had spent hours training him on how to use them. Interestingly, turned out Conor was a natural.

Of course, he wasn't there to kill anyone, but that didn't mean these people would surrender peacefully. The team had to be prepared for any possibility, and considering the severity of Brower's crimes, he doubted anyone in his group wished to be caught.

"Sixty seconds."

Conor took a moment to glance at the building where Gunner was positioned. Even though he couldn't see him, Conor knew his lover was watching over him. He reached for the dog tag under his shirt and held it tight. When he let go, Conor focused on the building. The sooner they got rid of the trash they could all go home. Well, in Conor's case, he could go find Jason.

"Spencer has control of the facilities," Brick said. "Five, four, three, two, go, go, go."

Conor ran to the side of the building with an exterior door. With a few practiced moves, he picked the lock on the side door, allowing him, Fletch, Shaw, and two FBI agents inside. They began working their way across the first floor as other units checked in over their comms. Room by room was cleared, and they had yet to run into any resistance, but other teams weren't so lucky.

Gunfire erupted from the other side of the building, but they were already committed, and as soon as they found the stairwell, they headed for the third floor to cut off anyone trying to flee. The moment they opened the third-floor stairwell door, bullets began ricocheting off the metal.

"Shit. We need to secure the floor. One at a time, we need to make it over to the first office," Fletch said while pointing at a hallway roughly five feet away. "We'll keep them busy while one of your agents rushes across."

The FBI agent nodded, and just as they were about to open the door to return fire, Conor felt the need to stop him. He grabbed on to the agent before he had a chance to make it out the door at the same time a hail of bullets rained down outside of it.

"Wait," Conor stated, and the agent stopped, but looked confused.

"I'd listen to him if you want to make it out of here in one piece," Shaw said.

He waited for the feeling to leave, and he released the agent. "Go."

When they opened the door, no one was firing on them, and the guy got out without a scratch. Conor, Shaw, and Fletch shot off a few rounds as the second agent went across, making the suspects duck for cover.

"Our turn," Fletch said.

"You two first. I can stop you if anything is off," Conor said.

"Okay, let's go," Shaw said.

Before long, there was no one left in the stairwell but him, and he was about to run into the offices when he heard a door above him close. He couldn't help but wonder if someone had been waiting for them to leave the stairwell before opening the door, and when Conor had been silent, they must've thought all of them were gone.

"I have a door closing above me. I'm going to check it out," Conor said softly, knowing they would hear him over the microphone.

"Be careful," Fletch said.

"I intend to."

He heard another round of shots fired on the third floor, but knew he had to keep going up. He pushed his back against the wall and carefully looked up the next flight of stairs. It appeared empty, but appearances could be deceiving. Step by step, he headed up, carefully checking to make sure no one came up behind him.

When he reached the fourth floor, he knew it wasn't the right one and kept going until he reached the door leading to the roof. The door must've bounced open, and he took the chance to peek out the crack, but saw no one. He used the tip of his rifle and nudged it open, expecting some reaction. When there wasn't so much as a peep, he crouched low and stepped out onto the dark roof.

Like other large multi-use buildings, there were large box-shaped machines bolted down on the roof containing what he guessed were the heat and air conditioning systems.

They were blocking his view.

"Gunner, see anyone on the roof?" Conor asked.

"Only you, but there are a lot of hidey-holes up there. I have your back."

Conor knew someone was up there with him. The question was who. There was only one way to make sure. With every move thought out five steps ahead, Conor went on the hunt. As he moved farther to the south side of the building, he heard talking, but the roof compressor was too loud for him to make out what was being said.

"Spence, can you turn off the compressor on the roof?"

"You got it," Spence answered, and in a few moments, it got quieter.

As soon as he could make out the words, he stopped.

"Rocko, where's that damn helicopter?"

It was Brower, and he seemed to be arranging a helicopter escape.

"Thirty seconds is too long. Get your ass down here and pick me up."

"Gunner, you hear that?" Conor whispered.

"Yeah. I'm changing locations to get a better angle."

More gunshots rang out below, but Conor continued to concentrate on the sound of Brower's footsteps on the gravel roofing, and realized something important.

"He's not alone." There were two distinct sets of steps.

"Can you see who it is?" Gunner asked.

Conor edged his way around the corner to try to take a better look.

"Shit. It's Devon."

"Devon?" Harris asked.

"Yeah. His hands are tied behind his back, and his mouth is taped shut. It looks like he's gone a few rounds."

"That bastard," Harris growled.

"We're on our way. Wait for backup," Brick said. "Harris, stay where you are."

Brower turned to look at Devon. "See where being a good cop leads? You should've given me the information I wanted on your partner and that team. All you had to do was tell me their location. Now, I no longer need you."

Brower raised his handgun and pointed it at Devon's head.

"Damn it," Conor growled and broke cover with his rifle pointing straight at Brower's head. "Put down your weapon."

Brower spun around and pulled Devon in front of him, using the man as a human shield. Conor wasn't surprised by the move. It was a coward's way.

"If it isn't one of those assholes now." Brower laughed. "I'll shoot him. Back off."

"No, you won't," Conor said. "Or I'll shoot you."

More gunfire broke out below.

"Under fire," Brick stated.

That meant it would take longer for them to get to him. He was responsible for saving Devon's life and stopping Brower from escaping.

"What do you think you're accomplishing here?" Brower yelled.

"I'm going to stop you from leaving," Conor answered. "And put you in prison."

"Well, I guess we don't need this asshole any longer," Brower said as he pushed the gun into Devon's temple.

"Wait, no. Don't kill him," Conor said as he raised the muzzle of his gun to point up in the air.

"You're soft. Put your rifle on the ground," Brower ordered with a slash of a grin across his face.

"Don't you do it," Gunner said in his ear.

"Trust me," Conor whispered.

The sound of a helicopter was getting closer, and Conor could see its lights moving across the sky.

"I can't get a shot off," Gunner said. "Devon's in the way."

"My ride is here." Brower laughed. "You and your team lose, but don't feel bad, you aren't in the same league I am."

Conor laid his rifle on the gravel and took a second to slide one of the throwing knives into his right hand. Brower was so busy watching Rocko fly closer that he didn't notice Conor swing his arm back and let the knife fly.

The blade hit its mark straight through Brower's wrist as he cried out in pain and dropped his gun. Devon took the opportunity to kick it away and run toward Conor, who pulled Devon behind the wall as Brower retrieved his gun with his left hand.

Conor released Devon from the zip ties around his wrists and removed the tape over his mouth. "Thanks, man. Am I glad to see you."

"Stay down, and we might get out of this alive."

"Fuck you," Brower screamed from somewhere behind them before firing his gun wildly with what was obviously not his dominant hand.

Conor heard bullets ricocheting off the walls, and then he heard one hit something metallic. He pulled his handguns from their holsters. He couldn't let Brower get away, and went around the corner with guns raised to see smoke billowing from the back of the helicopter. That had been the metal sound he'd heard. Brower had shot his getaway vehicle out of the sky.

As the chopper was forced to land, Conor gave Brower one last chance. "Put the gun down," he ordered.

Brower turned, raised his gun, and almost instantaneously, the asshole was lying on the gravel with a bullet wound to his leg. *Gunner.*

Conor rushed over and knocked Brower's gun away. Conor heard footsteps and turned to see the team rushing onto the roof. He'd wait until he could be with Gunner to take a deep breath.

Gunner had told him a while ago that Conor had saved his life, but now he had to wonder who saved whom.

***

Gunner

Finally, they were packing the hell up to head back to Fire Lake. Nine days felt like a couple of years away from Ben, but that was drawing to an end. Now, Reza had to give Conor Jason's info, and they were headed to court in two days. While everything wasn't riding on Jason, Conor felt certain finding Ben's father and having him testify would be the weight they'd need to win at the hearing. As for Brower, he was tucked away from society with a few new scars to show for his efforts to be anything but the outstanding citizen he pretended to be.

Neither the knife Conor had thrown nor the bullet Gunner had fired were kill shots, so the asshole would stand trial. The feds had him, and Gunner felt sure they would put him away for the rest of his life.

Rocko, the steadfast right-hand man, sang like a canary to save his ass, and Devon didn't suffer any lasting injuries from his time spent in captivity.

Harris had decided to return with the team to the lake house, and they'd begin searching for his sister once they were settled in.

The clients Brower had been meeting with turned out to be representatives of North Korea, even though, big surprise, the country denied any knowledge of their existence.

One unexpected item: Mrs. Brower had yet to be found. She emptied one of her bank accounts the day of the raid, and no one had seen her since. Her behavior indicated she knew what her husband was doing and jumped ship like a rat.

They'd catch her soon enough.

CHAPTER TWENTY-FOUR

Conor

Conor looked down at his phone to read the text message from an unknown number.

Jason Wells

8916 Welsh Drive

Hood River, Oregon

A picture of Ben's bio father was attached, and Conor could see the resemblance. Their noses and jaws were almost identical, and both had a small birthmark beside their left eyes. It wasn't big, but it was there.

They'd returned to the lake house last night, and while being with Ben had been heaven, waiting for Reza to get off his ass and give Conor Jason's address had been sheer torture.

Now that he had it, Conor knew he needed to leave immediately. He started looking for flights from the nearest airport, which was San Antonio and two hours away from Fire Lake, to Hood River, which was a little more than an hour away from Portland, OR. He found one flight that was leaving in four hours, and booked it, knowing they'd have to drive like maniacs to get to the airport on time.

He walked to the cottages under construction looking for Gunner and saw Gator was helping, as he often did. Gator began regaling one of his stories, which Conor didn't have time for, but he laughed along with Gator when Gunner came along and put his arm across Conor's shoulder.

Gator wore a crooked grin when he said, "I wasn't hitting on him, Gunner. I've already been warned."

Gunner nodded and said, "As long as it stays that way."

Shaking his head at Gunner's possessive nature, Conor flicked his fingers at Gator, took Gunner's hand and led him back to the lake house, to tell him the plan. When Gunner's phone pinged, he stood on the deck to take the call.

As Conor walked into the kitchen, Julia stopped him with a hand on his arm. "You look like you've seen a ghost," she said. "What's up?"

"I have to go."

Her head jerked back and she said, "Excuse me?"

"I have to leave immediately."

She moved in front of him. "If you leave Gunner two days before the court date, I'll cut off your balls and shove them down your throat."

"Ewww. What the hell?"

"I mean it. I never thought you'd be a love-him-and-leave-him type."

"I'm not. You don't understand."

"Then clear it up for me."

Spence walked in and took a look at the two of them. "What'd you do to piss off Julia?"

Before Conor could answer, Julia said, "He's leaving."

Spence's expression changed, but not in the way Julia likely expected.

"You found him?"

"Yeah."

"You want backup?"

"No. I don't want to scare him off."

"What the hell are you two talking about?" Julia asked.

Conor turned to Julia. "We've found Ben's bio father."

Julia looked between him and Spence before saying, "I hope you're right about that guy helping his son."

"Tell Gunner I'll be up in my room packing."

***

Gunner

Gunner walked into the lake house saw Julia and before she could say a word, he called out, "Conor?"

"Bedroom," Conor yelled from upstairs.

Gunner reached the top of the stairs and walked straight into Conor's bedroom to find him stuffing a duffle bag with clothing.

"You have the address?" he asked, already knowing the answer.

Conor spun around. "Man, we have to work on that bell."

"You didn't answer my question."

"Yep. I'll meet you guys at the hearing."

"You're still sure about this?"

"Yeah. It's urgent we get Jason to the hearing. Trust me."

Gunner couldn't help but worry. There was so much riding on the decision of a judge who had talked to Ben all of fifteen minutes, and was used to weighing the social worker's report heavily. Gunner had no idea what shit the in-laws would spew, but he could guess, and it was sure to get ugly during the hearing. He wasn't a leap of faith kind of guy, and to rest any hope on a man who'd forfeited his parental rights seemed a stretch, but Gunner believed in Conor, and his man seemed to put stock in what Jason would have to say.

"I know it's a big to believe he'll come with me, but if it all pans out, I know it'll be worth it."

Gunner took a deep breath and tried to clear his mind from many years of experience telling him not to trust that things would work out. But Conor had kept his word from the beginning of this mess, and he had done nothing to make Gunner doubt him or his gift.

"Okay."

"Okay?"

"Yeah, okay. I trust you and believe in you and your gift. Do you think you'll make it back for the court date?"

"That's my intention."

"Then I'll see you there."

"Nothing, short of death would keep me away."

***

Conor

Thirteen hours later, Conor faced that possibility as he stared down a Glock pointed straight at his head.

"Who are you?" the angry, gun-wielding man demanded. "How'd you get into the shop?"

Conor was seriously second-guessing picking the lock, but time was of the essence. The furniture in the shop looked hand carved and stunning, but he couldn't dwell on them right now. He had a boy to save.

"My name is Conor O'Brian, and I'm looking for Jason Wells."

"At two fucking thirty in the morning? I don't know no Jason Wells, but I do know how to dial nine-one-one."

"Please, it's important. It's about his son," Conor pleaded, a last-ditch effort before he'd likely be locked up, ending his chance at finding the man in time. He looked the guy up and down and noted he was smaller than Conor. Although he didn't want to go that route, he knew he could take him. "I was told he was here."

"Look, I don't know what kinda messed up game you—"

"It's okay, John. I'll speak with him," a voice said from behind the enraged man.

Moments later, the man from picture Reza had sent stepped out from a shadowed doorway. "What do you want?"

"Your help."

"Then you've come to the wrong place. I'm no help to anyone."

"You are to your son. He needs you now more than ever."

"What do you know about him?" Jason asked, looking suspicious.

Conor's arms were getting sore. "Can we point the gun in another direction, please?"

Jason looked at the guy he called John. "It's okay."

Conor slowly lowered his arms. "Thank you. Do you know how hard it is to find you?"

"Not hard enough. What's wrong with Ben?"

"Mandy died and your parents are trying to take Ben away from Mandy's brother Gunner, who she named in her will as Ben's legal guardian."

Conor watched the play of emotions run across Jason's face. Shock, sadness, confusion, fear, and ultimately rage.

"Do you think I gave up my son without thinking about was best for him? What I did five years ago was done to save Ben from those bastards."

"Yeah, I thought there was more to the story. I wish you had time to process the whole custody battle story, but we're out of time. The custody hearing is tomorrow, and we're half a country away from where we need to be."

"I can help with that," John, the guy holding the gun, said with a grin.

It took over an hour before the three men sat in a small Gulf Stream jet on a small private airfield while John did his flight prechecks. A pilot for private clients, he was going to fly them from Oregon to an even smaller private airfield outside San Antonio, where the custody hearing was being heard. A colleague owned the property, and the flight would take more than four hours. Then there was the drive from the airfield, which was forty miles from San Antonio to the courthouse, and they were going to drive it during rush hour.

"We need to get moving," Conor said.

"We'll be in the air in under ten minutes," John assured.

Jason sat staring at the most recent picture of Ben on Conor's phone. "Is he happy with his uncle?"

"Oh yeah. They're really special together. Gunner adores Ben who's the happiest, safest kid with his uncle and the team."

"Team?"

"Gunner's Navy SEALs team. They're retired, and have this beautiful property by a lake outside a small, storybook-looking town."

"It sounds wonderful."

"It is." *And he hoped he'd make it back there in one piece.*

All that mattered now was making it back to Texas in time to stop a potential miscarriage of justice.

As the small plane roared to life, Conor closed his eyes and hoped they'd get there in time.

CHAPTER TWENTY-FIVE

Gunner

The courtroom was cold and unyielding. Ben was sitting in another room with Julia and Matthew while his team members, Conor's grandmother, Uncle Marty, and Aunt Viv sat behind them, making their support known. A few of the old fishing crew and Gator had showed up and sat next to Conor's relatives. No one had heard from Conor, and court was reconvening after a short break. The social worker had already given his testimony, which turned out to be a glowing report of the care Gunner provided to his nephew and the wonderful life they lived together. One point for the good guys.

Still no Conor, and court was back underway. Gunner's attorney put him on the stand and took him through his military career, and how and why he gave it up when his sister died and he was named Ben's guardian. They went through the daily routine at the lake house, made Gunner talk about how much support was available to Ben, and how he had built-in child care, plus Ben had a best friend his own age who was part of the lake house support system.

When the in-laws' attorney began his cross-examination, his first question told Gunner everything he needed to know about the underhanded shit these people would employ to make him look unfit.

"Mr. Dobransky, do you enjoy killing people?"

"Objection, your honor," Gunner's lawyer, Ms. Ruiz, stated. "My client was a member of an elite Navy SEALs unit before retiring and deserves respect for his many years of service to his country."

"Sustained. The court deeply respects all those who have and continue to serve our great nation. The question will be struck from the record. Continue, counselor, and mind yourself."

Gunner looked over at the opposing lawyer, who didn't look as cocky as he did a moment ago. It seemed his attorney was as good as Roman said she was, which gave Gunner a moment of hope. Until the next question.

"Mr. Dobransky, you live in a house full of men, correct?"

"They're my SEALs team, my friends, and support system. They care about Ben as well."

"But they're all gay."

Ms. Ruiz stood and called out, "Objection. Mr. Dobransky's sexuality and those of the other Navy SEALs is not germane to this proceeding, your honor. If I may remind the court, the minor child was named as Mr. Dobransky's legal guardian at the behest of his sister, as was so stated in her lawful and correct last will and testament."

As the lawyers argued the validity of the question, Gunner noticed the back door to the courtroom open enough to allow Conor and Jason Wells to slip in. Gunner's spirits lifted, and he watched as the team followed his lead and turned around.

Watching the room, he saw Mrs. Wells's eyes get wide when she looked back, and she immediately whispered something into her husband's ear. The man didn't bother to look, but his demeanor changed instantly. He was no longer sitting back acting as if he was enjoying the show.

This could go one of two ways. Either Jason would petition for custody of his son now that he was the only living biological parent, or he could back Gunner's bid to keep Ben.

Then it hit him: what if Jason decided to back his parents instead?

Everything had changed, and suddenly the in-laws were asking for another recess, and Gunner was out of the hot seat.

Once he left the witness stand, he moved quickly to Conor and pulled him into his arms. Calm filled him instantly as Conor hugged him hard.

"I missed you," Conor said.

"I missed you too. I see you brought a friend. Hello, Jason," Gunner said before holding out his hand to the man.

Jason took it without hesitation. "Hello, Gunner. I'm sorry to hear my family is causing you all these problems. I thought I'd handled any potential interference by signing away my rights. I see I underestimated them." He grabbed Gunner's arm. "I can't tell you how sorry I am about Mandy. She was the best person I ever had the honor of knowing."

"Thanks. Is there anything you can do to help?"

"Excuse me. We'd like to talk with our son," an angry voice called from behind Conor.

They turned to find the in-laws and their lawyer standing a few feet away.

By now, the team had joined them and created quite an impressive wall, and even Gator came over to stand on the other side of Jason. Ms. Ruiz popped up to stand between the two opposing forces.

"No," she said on Jason's behalf. "He's our witness." Someone must've told her who he was and why he was here.

"You can't bring in last-minute witnesses," opposing counsel stated.

"That's for the judge to decide."

"Everyone return to their seats," the court clerk ordered, then the door adjacent to the courtroom opened. "All rise for the Honorable Judge Reume."

Ms. Ruiz didn't get a chance to speak with Jason before Gunner was forced to return to the witness stand to answer more messed-up questions. He prayed his sister was looking down on them and sending them luck. They needed it.

As soon as Gunner took his seat, the two attorneys approached the bench and were back to arguing.

The moment Ms. Ruiz told the judge Ben's biological father was present and wished to testify, opposing counsel went off the deep end. It felt like they were speaking a different language with all the legal terms, cases, and laws being thrown at the judge.

Gunner sat there listening, frustrated, and lost.

"As Mr. Jason Wells is Ben's biological father, and his whereabouts were discovered only early this morning, I believe his insight into this matter is warranted. Especially since he signed away his parental rights. I'll allow him to testify."

Gunner let out a deep breath he hadn't realized he'd been holding.

"Step back, both of you." The attorneys went to their respective tables. Then the judge said to opposing counsel, "You may continue with cross-examining Mr. Dobransky."

***

Conor

He watched as the in-laws' lawyer tried to rile Gunner with questions that sought to portray him as a monster. Conor had to smile. Clearly, they didn't know who they were dealing with. No one, especially some up-his-own-ass suit, would break Gunner. He'd spent his life fighting bigger badasses in his sleep. After thirty interminable minutes, the shithead lawyer finally gave up and ended his questioning.

Conor never took his eyes off Gunner as he returned to his seat beside Ms. Ruiz, who stood and said, "We call Mr. Jason Wells to the stand."

Conor looked over at Jason and said the obvious, "Do what's best for Ben."

Jason made his way to the witness stand and promised to tell the truth. Unfortunately, Conor wasn't sure what that truth was because

Jason hadn't said a word about his parents, or anything else for that matter, throughout the whole flight to Texas. All he'd wanted to know was more about his son, and Conor told him everything he knew. Jason soaked up all the information like a starving man, making Conor wonder why he'd given away his parental rights in the first place.

"Could you please state your name?"

"Jason Benjamin Wells."

Conor wondered if that was how Ben got his name.

"And you are Benjamin Dobransky's biological father."

"Yes."

"Objection. He relinquished his rights when Ben was born," the in-laws' lawyer argued.

"Overruled. As counsel well knows, relinquishing rights does not negate his status as the boy's biological father."

"I'm lodging a continuing objection to the witness."

"So noted," the judge said. "Ms. Ruiz, please continue your direct examination of the witness."

"Thank you, your honor. Jason, why did you give up your parental rights to Ben?'

"Because I wanted what was best for him."

"Explain that."

"Mandy and I were young and best friends. She was an angel and knew all my secrets. She'd always been there for me, and I loved her. One night, we got drunk and one thing led to another. Mandy knew I was gay before I was ready to admit it. She wanted me to be part of Ben's life, to be his dad. Other than sending them money, I couldn't do that to my boy. Not with the way my parents are. Mandy knew about them and understood."

"What do you mean by 'the way my parents are'?"

"We were responsible parents," Mr. Wells growled from behind the petitioners' table.

"Counsel, control your client, and sir, do not interrupt these proceedings again," the judge warned, then he made a hand motion and said, "Ms. Ruiz."

"They were exceptionally cold and distant through most of my life. At least until I became a teenager."

"And what happened when you became a teenager?"

"I came out to them. I honestly thought they wouldn't care, but I was wrong."

"They did care?"

"Who wouldn't?" Mr. Wells interrupted once again. The sneer on his face told the whole story.

"Sir, you've been warned," the judge stated firmly. "One more outburst and I'll hold you in contempt of court and have you removed from my courtroom."

Opposing counsel stood. "Sorry, your honor. It won't happen again."

"Please answer the question." The judge motioned to Jason.

"They were upset and began yelling that I was an aberration and an affront to them and society. They were worried about how they'd look to their friends at the country club, and how it would ruin the family reputation."

"Did it end there?" Ms. Ruiz asked.

"No. They put me in a conversion camp where gay kids are sent to make them straight."

"How long were you there?"

"Which time?"

"How many times were you sent away to the camp?"

"Five times."

"Were they all the same camp?"

"No. The first four were the usual 'hate yourself for being gay' courses meant to change your mind. As if being gay was a choice."

"What happened at the last one that was different?

"This facility was in a different state, and if anyone knew about the methods they employed, they'd be locked up in prison."

"Please explain."

"Beatings, sleep deprivation, food deprivation, being shocked by cattle prods—"

Mr. Wells stood up, and his attorney tried to push him down, but the old bastard wasn't having any of it. He leaned forward and shouted, "They did what they had to. Nothing else was working."

The judge opened his mouth, but Jason got there first.

"This," Jason ground out as he stood and pulled his shirt over his head and spun around to reveal his mutilated back. "This is what you had them do to me."

There was a collective gasp and groan from the gallery. Conor was as shocked as everyone else. And boy, was he glad Ben wasn't in the room. The amount and type of damage done to create grooves in the thick scarring was incomprehensible. Some of the scars were a dark, angry red, while others were white from layers of scar tissue that'd built up over repeated whippings and beatings.

And Jason wasn't done. He turned and glared at his parents. "And the scars don't stop there. If you allow them to have custody of Ben, this is the life you're condemning my son to. I tried to protect him from them by giving him up. Do you think I wanted to walk away from my son? My precious boy? I sure as hell did not. But as his father, my first priority was to protect him. And protecting him from them was paramount. Under no circumstances were they going to do to him what they did to me, or bring him up to believe doing such horrible things to anyone because they are gay was all right." He pulled on his shirt and turned to the judge. "I beg you not to remove Ben from his uncle's care."

Mr. Wells ran around the petitioners' table and charged the witness stand, trying to get at Jason. The court bailiff stopped the crazy, deranged man at the same time more officers flooded the courtroom as the judge, his clerk, and the court reporter got away through the door beside the judge's bench.

Conor ran to Gunner, who latched on to him as the elder Wells, who was screaming at Jason, "They should've killed you," was escorted from the courtroom by two officers as Mrs. Wells followed behind them. Their lawyer sat in his chair, shaking his head.

"You knew there was more to this. That's why you searched for Jason," Gunner said. "My sister never told me the whole story."

"Ben is safe, and you'll raise him as your sister wanted. That's all that matters."

Before Gunner could ask more questions, Ms. Ruiz came over with Jason by her side and said, "We need to talk. Let's regroup at your hotel."

Conor stepped a few feet away so they could speak, but Gunner pulled him back in. "You're my partner in all things. We face this together."

CHAPTER TWENTY-SIX

Gunner

Julia, Matthew, and Ben were in a suite across the hall. Gunner left the boys playing with their new Transformers. Knowing the stress and trauma the hearing caused Ben, Gunner made sure to have a surprise waiting for him when they returned to the hotel.

While Gunner had been talking to Ben, Jason stood in the hall doorway watching but made no move to approach or speak to him. But that didn't mean he didn't want to. Gunner could see it in his eyes. He wasn't sure how he felt about Jason being around Ben, but if everything he'd said was true, Jason deserved a chance to get to know his son.

Something else to deal with, to "process" on top of all the other shit they'd put up with that day.

Ms. Ruiz escorted Jason to the hotel lobby so he could get a room, and with them out of the room, Gunner relaxed slightly.

They had the penthouse suite, and everyone was standing in the large living room with newfound hope. There was no way the judge would remove Ben from Gunner's care, not after what happened in the courtroom.

There was a knock on the door. "Now what?" Gunner growled.

He heard the door open and recognized the voice before she entered the room. Ms. Ruiz followed Brick into the living room. She took stock of everyone's stance, and said, "I had a call from the court clerk and a fax waiting for me at the front desk." A few brows went up as she sat on the sofa in front of the coffee table and pulled out a piece of paper from her briefcase.

"So?" Gunner asked.

"Even if this new information hadn't come to light, Mr. Wells's outbursts were getting on the judge's last nerve. But with Jason's testimony, coupled with Mr. Wells trying to attack his son in open court, the judge has terminated proceedings and has entered an order."

"We won?" Conor asked. "Ben can stay with us?"

"Yes," she said with a big smile.

The room erupted into cheers, slaps on the back, and fist bumps. Then Gunner went to Ms. Ruiz and said, "Thank you. Really. You can't know what this means to me."

As she smiled, another knock came at the suite's door. Spencer checked the peephole, opened it, and Julia came inside, Matt and Ben right behind her. Both boys had their backpacks on and were holding their new Transformers.

"I heard cheering and thought maybe we could join you."

"Come in. Ben is staying with his Uncle Gunner," Brick announced.

The boys came running into the suite's living room, and Gunner picked up Ben and spun him around.

"I get to stay with you?"

"Yeah, kid. You're not going anywhere."

Ben wrapped his little arms around Gunner's neck and buried his face there. When Conor went to step away, Gunner pulled him into their hug. This was his family, and no one was ever going to mess with it again.

As the cheering died down, Ms. Ruiz said, "There's one matter that requires resolution. The judge wants to meet with Ben's father."

The room quieted, and Ben's head came up out of Gunner's neck. "Father?"

Ms. Ruiz's mouth dropped open. "I'm so sorry."

"Mommy said my dad loved me."

"He does, little man," Gunner said softly. "Would you like to meet him?"

"My dad is here?" Ben asked.

"Yeah."

"Can I see him?"

"If you want to."

Ms. Ruiz took out her phone. "Hey. C'mon up to the penthouse suite. Someone wants to meet you." She nodded, said, "Yes," and then touched the phone's screen. "He'll be here in a few minutes."

Gunner sat on the couch and slid Ben next to him. "Okay, buddy. You do and say what you feel like doing and saying. Nothing's right and nothing's wrong. Got it?"

The boy nodded. "I got it."

Spencer had stayed by the suite's door and answered the knock immediately. Jason walked into the room and looked directly at Ben.

Gunner stood. Ben followed and took Gunner's hand.

"Ben, I'd like you to meet your dad."

Now that the two were side by side, the similarities between father and son were glaring.

"Hello, Ben," Jason whispered. "I've waited a long time to meet you again."

"Again?" Ben asked.

"I was there the day you were born," Jason said.

"Did you get lost?"

Jason took a deep breath and closed his eyes, looking far older than his years.

"Yes. I've been lost for a long time," Jason explained, and Gunner understood all too well what the man meant.

"Do you want to see my Transformers?"

"I'd love to."

The brave little dude reached up, took hold of Jason's hand, and led him over to the couch. Ben reached into his backpack and pulled out the first of his many robot toys and lined them up next to the newest one.

"This is Bumblebee. He's my favorite."

"I think he's one of the best on the team," Jason said as he fought back the tears.

"Why are you sad, Daddy?"

"I'm not sad, Ben. These are happy tears. Do you think I can have a hug?" Jason asked tentatively.

Ben didn't stop to think about it, he raised his arms. The two hugged for a couple of minutes, Jason's happiness unmistakable.

Gunner waited for the pain to start, for the worry of losing Ben to begin, but it never came. Having Ben's father in his life was the right move for Ben and Jason. The man had already given up so much to protect his son.

He knew his sister would be happy with this result, and Gunner couldn't help but smile at the thought.

***

"Ready to go?" Conor asked as he stood in the doorway.

Gunner's lover had been the only one to keep him sane these last couple of months. He didn't know what he would've done without Conor.

"More than ready."

He grabbed his bag off the bed and threw it over his shoulder. They'd be home in a little more than four hours. He couldn't wait.

Conor met him in the middle of the room and draped his arms over Gunner's shoulders. "My grandma would say you never know how much you miss something until it's gone."

"Your grandmother's a smart lady."

"She'll be happy to hear you said that." Conor smiled. "Now give me a kiss, handsome, and take me and Ben home."

"How could I say no to that?" Gunner kissed his lover, his everything.

Their time together had been a whirlwind, but they'd rounded the last and most important corner.

They'd come from a place of distrust and anger and were able to find their way together and build a new life out of a shaky past. The grumpy Navy SEALs sniper and the private investigator from New York made a solid team after all.

Gunner's phone rang, and he answered without looking.

"Yep."

"Gunner, it's Elias." Alarm bells started sounding. "There's been a development. I've received a message. Frank and Lisa Wells have vanished."

"Did someone contact Jason?" Conor asked, having heard what the sheriff had said. "The way Frank looked at his son, Jason might be in danger."

Gunner placed the call on speaker.

"Yeah. He's safe. Gator got him from the hotel, and they're on their way to Marshall where they'll hunker down until his parents are found." Gunner wanted to ask how and why Gator was involved, but there were more important things in play here.

"Why would those assholes disappear?" he asked. They hadn't heard anything about them after learning the old man was charged with attempted battery, and had been released on bail.

"From what I'm reading, they're wanted for embezzling money from the country club where they sat on the board as CFO and president. After news of his courtroom tirade went wide, Frank was removed from the board, and that's when some board members noticed the discrepancies in the books."

"Does it say how much they stole?" Gunner asked.

"North of eight hundred thousand dollars," Elias said.

"Not only homophobes, but thieves as well. I'm more thankful than ever Ben has and will have no contact with them," Conor said.

"Same." Gunner pulled Conor into his arms.

"They won't last long with the Feds after them," Elias said.

"Feds? Wouldn't their crime be at a state level?" Gunner asked.

"You'd think, but financial donations to a wounded warrior program have gone missing as well. They sit on that board, and the program is incorporated in a different state than the country club and where they reside. Now it looks like their thievery is multi-state."

"Assholes," Gunner muttered.

"They got no shame. After what they did to Jason, I shouldn't be surprised by anything those two do," Conor said.

Gunner hung up the phone. "Let's get Ben home."

"Agreed. Fire Lake is where I want to be with my family."

Gunner pulled Conor even closer. "I'll never get tired of hearing you say that."

"I'll never get tired of saying it."

Gunner dove in for a kiss to seal the deal.

This was the life he never knew he wanted, and he'd never take it for granted.

CHAPTER TWENTY-SEVEN

Jason

Jason liked the bar most when it was like this. Quiet with the wood gleaming in the setting sun, all the tables clean and ready for the doors to open and for neighbors to walk in. Jason had been working on a new piece of furniture designed to add more shelving behind the bar, and it was coming along nicely.

Gator had been a wonderful host while Jason was hiding out. His psycho parents were still on the loose, and he wanted to make sure he never saw them again.

Gator had given Jason the spare bedroom in the two-bedroom apartment above the bar. By way of thanks for taking him in, Jason occasionally helped around the bar.

The apartment was large and relatively modern compared to the bar. Gator said it was because people felt more comfortable in a space they recognized. They knew what to expect and could settle in and relax, which were only two of his reasons for not remodeling the downstairs.

Over the past few weeks, Jason had the opportunity to visit with Ben at Fire Lake, and he treasured every moment. He never thought he'd have a relationship with his son, but thanks to Gunner and Conor, he was now part of Ben's life.

Jason looked down at the tan leather bracelet Ben had made for him. Ben had etched "DAD" into the leather, and Jason had cried when his son gave it to him.

Ben was an amazing kid. Smart and kind like his mother. It was still hard to believe Mandy was gone. But he saw her in their son whenever he looked at Ben.

Jason knew when Ben got older, he'd learn and understand what really happened, and why Jason gave up his parental rights. It wouldn't be easy for the boy to look past what Jason had done, but he hoped someday he'd find it in his heart to forgive his father for taking what would seem like the easy way out.

Of all the surprises that'd changed Jason's life, Gator was one of the biggest. He was an amazing man who helped people around town, and always had a minute to stop and talk to someone. He always made the person he talked with feel like they were the only one in the world, and many people came to him for advice. He never turned anyone away.

Jason had caught himself more than once wishing Gator was gay. The fact he had an ex-wife didn't nix the possibility, but it lowered the likelihood by a lot.

Jason had met a lot of men who were gay but had married for a variety of reasons. Not the least of which was to cover their truth. From what Jason could see, the small Texas town of Marshall wasn't what he'd call forward thinking or liberal. Some people were, but most, not so much. But there was a level of tolerance that made living here doable. It wasn't the East or West Coasts, but he'd met many fine, decent people.

As for Gator, it didn't matter if he was gay. The guy was great, and Jason would make sure the piece he created for the bar fit the unique man it was being made for.

He'd used black walnut to build the shelving unit. It was strong and had a dense grain, which made it perfect for the bar. The dark chocolate color would make quite a statement at the back of the bar, with bottles of the finer liquors stored and displayed on its shelves.

What had first begun as a couple of extra shelves had turned into a full-fledged installation at the end of the bar with shelving, cabinets, an inlaid mirror and intricate carvings. It was going to be stunning when completed.

He had to admit it felt odd being in the bar by himself. Gator had gone to pick up a beef delivery from Bryan for the bar's restaurant. The cook was amazing and came with the place when Gator had bought it. Six employees worked at the bar. Jason had met and liked them all. It felt like a family of sorts.

He took one final look at his work in progress and began packing away his tools. Various chisels, carving knives, gauges, a hand saw, clamps, a smoothing plane, and more filled the old leather doctor's bag he'd found at a swap meet years ago. It was large, black, and worn around the edges, which was perfect for his needs. People threw too many things away these days, even when there was lots of life left in them.

He didn't have all his tools, they were back in Hood River, but he'd had a few things shipped down he'd needed to complete the project.

John, his best friend and business partner, was running the furniture store while Jason was away. Soon he'd be moving to Marshall full time to be near Ben, and he'd asked John if he wanted to relocate the store or have him ship pieces back to Oregon.

Jason was still waiting for an answer. He knew it was hard for his friend, having lived in Hood River all his life, but Jason was determined to be near his son, and nothing would keep him from Ben.

Of course, he'd never leave his friend high and dry, and assured John that no matter what he decided, Jason would continue to make pieces for the shop.

As he was about to put the last chisel away, he heard the floor creak and spun around to find his father standing on the other side of the bar. How the hell had he gotten in?

"Hello, son," the old man said.

Though the urge was strong, Jason stopped himself from shouting. He knew it would get him nowhere. He was alone. He had to buy time, and slid the chisel up his sleeve.

"Hello, Frank." *You crazy bastard.*

His father looked different from when he saw him in the courthouse. He was thinner, and looked a little pale, and a whole lot crazier.

"It took me some time to track you down," Frank said. "It was almost as if you were hiding from your father."

Okay.

"I've been working on a new project," Jason said, waving at the shelving unit behind him. *I need more time.*

"Well, I'm glad I found you. We need to talk, son," Frank said as he crossed his arms over his chest as he typically did when he was pissed off. *Shit.*

"Where's Mom?" She had to be around here somewhere. They'd run together.

"She couldn't handle the stress, buddy. You know your mother wasn't stable."

"Where is she?" Jason had a bad feeling, worse than the usual one he had when around Frank.

"All the running and hiding in cheap motels became too much for her," Frank said as if he were talking about the weather.

"Did Mom commit suicide?" Jason asked in a shaky voice.

"No. No, son." He shook his head.

Thank god. He didn't want anyone to die. All he wanted was to be left alone.

"I put her out of her misery."

"What?!" Jason wasn't sure he'd heard him correctly.

"You see, the bed linens were too scratchy, the room next door was too loud, the air conditioner was too cold, and the food was too basic for her. Your mother reminded me again and again how unhappy she was. So, being the good husband I am, I had to end her suffering."

Jason felt like throwing up, but he forced himself to remain still.

"What did you do?" he asked.

Frank couldn't be serious. Maybe she turned herself in, or he sent her away.

"She was in the bath, the water wasn't hot enough, and I put my hands on the top of her head."

"That's enough."

Jason was right. *A whole lot crazier.* The fuckin' bastard had lost his mind. He'd always been nuts, but after what happened in that courtroom, he must've felt unrestrained and unafraid to allow the real man to come out.

Whatever the case, odds were Jason was the next victim.

"Now we are here."

"Um, yeah, we are." Jason began backing out of the bar and toward the front doors. If he could get outside, he'd have a better chance of finding help.

Frank moved around the outside of the bar. "You should have listened to me," he said. "None of this would've happened if you'd been a normal boy."

"I am normal."

"Gay isn't normal," Frank yelled.

Right. Don't anger the crazy man.

"Would you like a drink? I could make you one." He didn't know the first thing about bartending. Maybe he should've grabbed a bottle as a weapon.

"Alcohol won't fix this, son."

"What will?"

"You, joining your mother. Don't worry. I'll be along shortly behind you. I'm sure the good lord will understand and forgive you your sins."

My sins? He was going to need some serious therapy after this.

"How about you go first?"

Jason was out from behind the bar and backing toward the front when he took his eyes off his father for a flash of a moment to check behind him for tables. When he glanced back, the psycho was gone.

Jason froze. Where was he?

For a fraction of a second, he thought maybe stress had gotten the better of him, and his brain had made the whole thing up. He immediately nixed that idea. The man was real, and he was in the bar somewhere.

Jason had to get out of here.

He turned to run for the doors when Frank came around the front, forcing him to turn back. He was facing his father again, but still backing away.

"Why can't you leave me alone?"

"Because I have to save you. I love you, son," Frank said with a toothy smile.

And here I thought he couldn't get creepier.

"The police will find you."

"It won't matter."

Right. Kill the son before the suicide.

He'd been living upstairs, and though he'd been in the bar quite a bit, he didn't have the layout down yet. He knew he was getting close to some tables, but wasn't sure where they were.

"You're making this harder than it has to be. I promise to make it quick, but I doubt it'll be painless."

Jason was terrified.

His father wasn't a big man, but from experience Jason knew maniacs got a strength surge when they were rampaging,

He also knew time was running out.

Gator, where are you?

ABOUT THE AUTHOR

M. Tasia is a M/M romance author who lives in Ontario, Canada. She's is a dedicated people watcher, lover of romance novels, 80's rock, and happily-ever-afters (once the MCs are put through their paces, of course), who grew up with a love of reading.

She's a firm believer that everyone deserves to have love, excitement, and crazy hot romance in their lives. Love should be celebrated and shared.

Connect with M.:
mtasiabooks.com
FB: mtasiabooks
twitter: @mtasiaauthor
IG: @m.tasia.author
TikTok: @mtasiauthor

www.BOROUGHSPUBLISHINGGROUP.com

If you enjoyed this book, please write a review. Our authors appreciate the feedback, and it helps future readers find books they love. We welcome your comments and invite you to send them to info@boroughspublishinggroup.com.

Follow us on Facebook, TikTok and Instagram, and be sure to sign up for our newsletter for surprises and new releases from your favorite authors.

Are you an aspiring writer? Check out www.boroughspublishinggroup.com/submit and see if we can help you make your dreams come true.

Love podcasts? Enjoy ours at:
www.boroughspublishinggroup.com/podcast

www.ingramcontent.com/pod-product-compliance
Lightning Source LLC
Chambersburg PA
CBHW030328180626
46810CB00003B/1276